THE COVENT GARDEN CAPER

TRACY GRANT

The Covent Garden Caper

Ebook ISBN: 9781641973502

POD ISBN: 9781641973564

NYLA Publishing

121 W 27th St., Suite 1201, New York, NY 10001

http://www.nyliterary.com

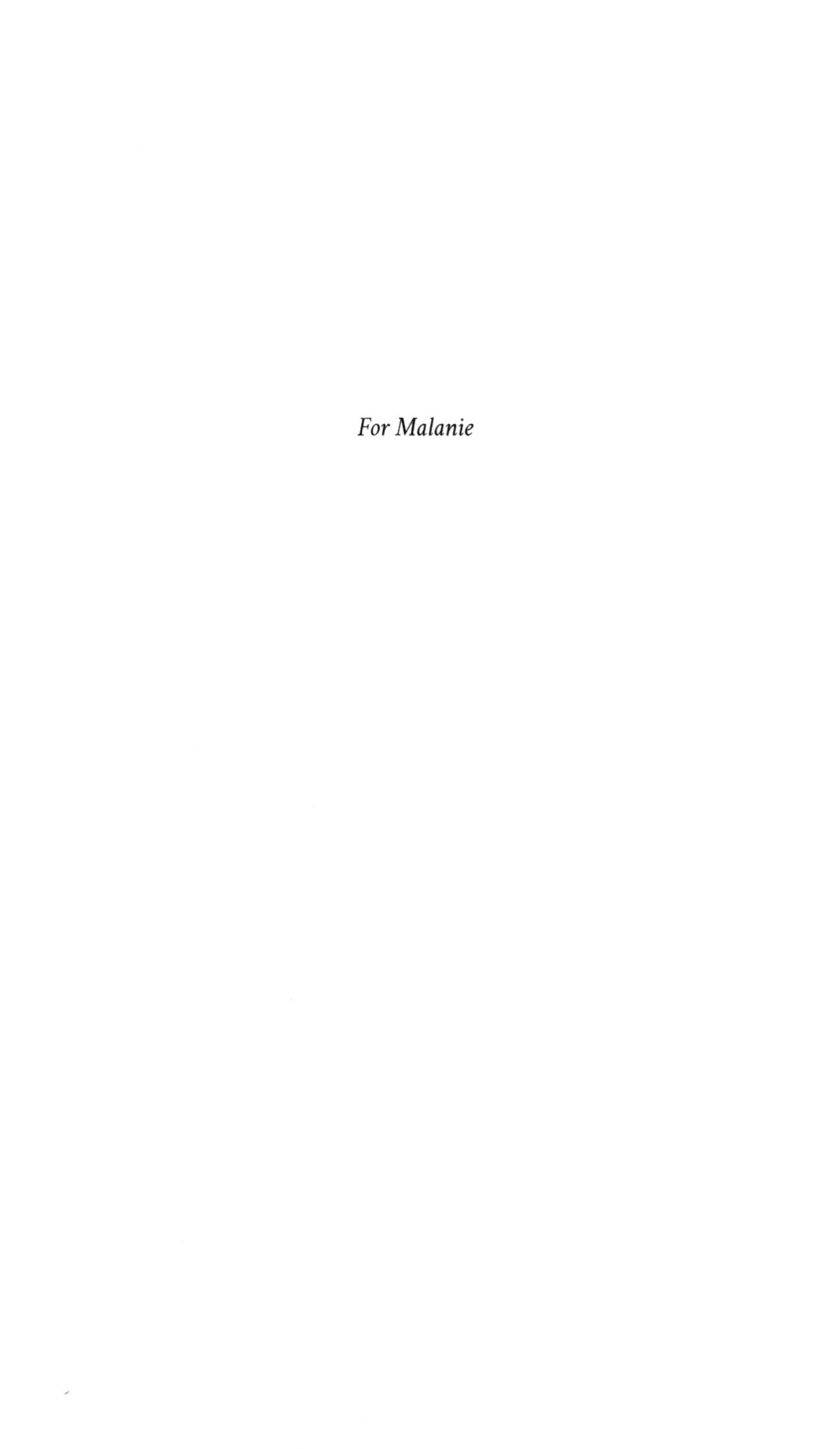

For Malanie

Give me some music—music, moody food
  Of us that trade in love.

— SHAKESPEARE, ANTONY & CLEOPATRA, ACT II,
SCENE V

DRAMATIS PERSONAE

*indicates real historical figures

<u>The Rannoch Family & Household</u>

Malcolm Rannoch, MP and former British intelligence agent
Mélanie Suzanne Rannoch, his wife, playwright and former
French intelligence agent
Colin Rannoch, their son
Jessica Rannoch, their daughter
Berowne, their cat

Laura O'Roarke, Colin and Jessica's former governess
Raoul O'Roarke, her husband, Mélanie's former spymaster, and
Malcolm's father
Lady Emily Fitzwalter, Laura's daughter from her first marriage
Clara O'Roarke, Laura and Raoul's daughter

Valentin, footman

<u>The Mallinson Family</u>

Julien (Arthur) Mallinson, Earl Carfax, former agent for hire
Katelina (Kitty) Velasquez Mallinson, Countess Carfax, his wife,
former British and Spanish intelligence agent
Leo Ashford, her son
Timothy Ashford, her son
Guenevere (Genny) Ashford, Kitty and Julien's daughter
Luna, their puppy

Hubert Mallinson, spymaster, Julien's uncle
Amelia Mallinson, his wife
Lucinda Mallinson, their daughter
David Mallinson, MP, their son
Simon Tanner, playwright, his lover

Bernard Devereux, Lucinda's childhood friend

Honoria Talbot Atwood, Hubert's niece
Gerald, her footman

The Davenport Family

Lady Cordelia Davenport, classicist
Colonel Harry Davenport, her husband, classicist, and former
British intelligence agent
Livia Davenport, their daughter
Drusilla Davenport, their daughter

Archibald (Archie) Davenport, Harry's uncle
Lady Frances (Fanny) Davenport, his wife, Malcolm's aunt
Chloe Dacre-Hammond, Frances's daughter

The Roth Family

Jeremy Roth, Bow Street runner

Judith Roth, his wife, Frances's daughter
Harriet Roth, Jeremy's sister
Tristram Gresham, composer and agent

The Southcott Family

Anthony (Tony) Southcott, Duke of Bamford
Désirée Clairineau, his mistress
Sophie, their daughter

Henrietta (Hetty) Southcott, Duchess of Bamford

John Southcott, Tony's nephew
Tom Elton, his valet
Maggie, his housemaid

Others

*Sir Nathaniel Conant, chief magistrate of Bow Street
*Lord Sidmouth, home secretary
*Lord Castlereagh (now Lord Londonderry), home secretary
*George IV

Bertram Caulfield-West, diplomat

Danielle Darnault, opera singer and agent

CHAPTER 1

London
July 1821

The tumblers clicked, then stuck. Mélanie Rannoch pressed her eye to the keyhole and jiggled the picklock again. Another click. Another pause. She maneuvered some more, waited for yet another click, maneuvered again. The lock clicked open. A decent challenge, but far from the most complex she'd faced. Over a decade in espionage—even if she continued to fool herself she was retired—did make lock picking a frequent occurrence.

A hand closed on her elbow. As usual, Julien moved soundlessly. Without speaking, without even audibly breathing, he helped her to her feet. She turned the handle and eased open the unlocked door.

Nothing stirred in the shadows beyond. She stepped into the room and sensed more than felt Julien move beside her over the smooth floorboards. No light except a sliver of moonlight filtered through the curtains. She could make out a dark mass that was probably a bed. Something white shone against one of the bedposts. A tall rectangle that was likely a wardrobe. A dressing table or writing desk near the windows. A carriage rattled by in the street below. Light from the carriage lamps streaked through a narrow gap.

"Curtains," Julien said."

She stepped forwards and nearly fell as her foot thudded into something that went skittering over the thick-piled rug (Axminster, likely). She moved to the window and pulled the curtains closed against any more betraying light. She tugged a pin from inside her bodice—always important to have one handy on a mission—and pinned the curtains closed. Julien, who seemed to be able to see in the dark, pulled a flint from his pocket and lit a lamp that stood on what was indeed a writing desk. Light flared and spilled over the room. The white blur tangled round the bedpost was a lace-edged chemise threaded through with pale blue ribbon. A wine glass had come to rest against the bed—probably what she had stumbled against and sent skittering across the rug when she came into the room. Lace-edged stays dangled over a blue velvet chair back.

"He certainly didn't tidy up before he left for the country," she said.

"More to the point, neither did his valet, who left town with him, if Raoul's intelligence is good. Which it usually is."

Julien turned to the writing desk. Polished mahogany. A tooled leather blotter, green with gilding, a chased silver pen and inkpot, a row of nibs, a stack of hot-pressed writing paper, a sealing wax set and several seals with different designs. Julien tugged open a drawer and began methodically riffling through the contents. Mélanie joined him and tried another drawer. Julien pulled out a stack of letters tied in buff ribbon, flipped through them, paused to read a few. "He has a flowery style. Most are written to an Annabel. I hope she appreciates his fondness for adjectives and atrocious use of adverbs. Doesn't appear to be anything useful though."

"Bills." Mélanie set down a stack of papers from her drawer. "Tailors, bootmakers. Hats, gloves. Champagne, claret, brandy. A large one from Asprey's for a sapphire necklace that may have been intended for the fair Annabel."

"Compensation for putting up with his literary efforts." Julien peered at one of the pages, held it to the lamplight. "Could any of them be in code?"

"I don't think so. Malcolm's taught me to recognize coded bills. They were very popular with agents in Vienna."

Julien tugged open a lower drawer that was deeper, and pulled out a dispatch box. Brass bound. "Looks like he may at least have had the wit to keep official papers locked up."

Mélanie pulled her picklocks out again. This lock was a bit easier than the one on the door. She pushed back the lid. A jumble of papers met their gaze. The Honorable Bertram Caulfield-West wasn't tidy in any part of his life, it seemed. She and Julien began going through the papers. "Foreign correspondents," Julien said. "This looks promising."

But the letter they were looking for wasn't there. "Could he have had the sense to burn it?" she said.

"Possibly. Though he doesn't seem possessed of a great deal of sense. It's also possible someone else discovered it first."

Mélanie met Julien's gaze, a host of disturbing possibilities shooting through her mind. "We haven't looked everywhere. Perhaps—"

She broke off at an owl cry from the street. Their agreed-upon warning with Kitty and Malcolm.

Julien met her gaze and of one accord they pushed the dispatch box back in the drawer and moved to the window. Footsteps sounded. Light but distinct. The stairs creaked, which had been a challenge when they broke in but was helpful now. She pulled the pin from the curtains and Julien pushed up the sash. The footsteps pattered closer. No room for doubt. They sprang through the window and landed on a ledge. Two storeys up. Too far to jump.

"Bertie!" A woman's voice screamed from inside the room. Julien jerked his head to the side. They lowered themselves onto an overhang five feet below and crouched against the stucco wall.

"Bertie!!" The woman yelled again, this time out the open window from the sound of it. "Who's with you?"

A rattle, as though she'd shaken the window frame, then retreating footsteps.

Julien glanced down the side of the building. Mélanie followed his gaze. Cream-colored stucco. Pavement below. Possible to land on hands and feet, but one couldn't count on it. "We wouldn't necessarily break anything."

"Not necessarily," Julien agreed. "But I've learnt caution since I've become a father." He looked at the next building over. It was a storey lower. "If we climb up to the roof and jump down to the next house over, there's an easier path down."

Mélanie was already pulling the ribbon from her chemise and kirtling up her gown.

A door banged open and shut in Sackville Street. "Bertie!" The woman's scream came from the street this time. On the opposite side of the house from where they crouched.

"Oh god," Julien said.

Pounding feet on the pavement.

"Now she's roused the watch," Mélanie said. "Malcolm and Kitty—"

"Can take care of themselves." Julien caught her hand. "We can do more on solid ground."

They climbed up, using the window frames and plaster decorations for foot- and-handholds, and pulled themselves onto the roof. Broken tiles cut through the sarcenet of her gown as they crawled over the roof, trying to keep to shadows away from the sightline of those in Sackville Street. For once she wished she had gloves on. Julien jumped down onto the lower roof next door and held out his hands to catch her as she sprang after. They leant against the stucco wall for a few moments. Nothing silent about either of their breathing now. Julien was right, the way down was easier thanks to all the embellishments. Ornate architecture had its uses. It was just that they were both more tired.

"Here, now." The deep voice came from the street. "What are you doing here?"

"He jumped." The woman's voice from earlier. "Out of a window. With a woman."

"Who did?"

"Right." Julien stretched his arms. "At least the path down is in shadow."

CHAPTER 2

Malcolm Rannoch leant back into the shadows between the neat rows of stucco houses. Most of them bachelor establishments, similar to those in which he himself had lived a decade ago. Before Mélanie and their children. Before he was a diplomat or a politician or a spy. In a life it was now hard to remember.

Kitty Mallinson was across the street in the shadows of a lamppost, keeping watch as he was. As Raoul was doing further down the street. Which was hardly necessary, given how skilled Mélanie and Julien were. Still, it was always imperative to have backup. They had all learnt that to their cost.

The street was quiet at this hour, the odd carriage rattling by, but little to disturb the pools of moonlight and lamplight on the blue-black pavement. Most of the denizens of Sackville Street were snug abed—or more likely out sampling the pleasures of the town. The occasional pedestrian heading out for the evening or returning home hadn't paid any heed to them.

A hackney clattered past and pulled up, three doors down. Two young men in silk hats ran down the steps of the house opposite and jumped into the hackney. Malcolm caught fragments of "sure to win tonight, feeling lucky" and "the fair Maria." The hackney rumbled off. Moments later, footsteps thudded from the opposite direction. A woman ran down the street, the hood of her dark blue cloak thrown back, guinea-gold ringlets tumbling over her shoulders. Making straight for the house where Bertram Caulfield-West lodged. Where Mélanie and Julien were in the midst of a break-in.

Kitty moved quickly to intercept the woman. "Dear ma'am, do be careful."

The blonde woman spun round to stare at Kitty. "Who are you? Were you with Bertie?"

"Bertie?" Kitty said. "Mr. Caulfield-West?"

"You *were* with him?" The blonde woman's voice rose with jealousy.

"Mr. Caulfield-West is away from town," Kitty said (quite truthfully, for all their intelligence). "But I've just been visiting the lodger on the ground floor, and I fear he has an infectious fever."

The blonde woman sprang back. "I don't believe you."

"I assure you it's true, madam." Malcolm sprang from the shadows and moved to Kitty's side. "My wife and I have just left our grievously ill friend's bedside. The doctor advises that no one enter the house."

The blonde woman dodged round Kitty and made for the door. "I won't go anywhere near his rooms."

"We've already been in the house and run the risk." Malcolm moved to put himself between the woman and the front door of the house. "If you would like us to deliver a message to Mr. Caulfield-West."

"Thank you. This is a message only I can deliver myself." The woman pushed against Malcolm's arm. Malcolm caught a handful of her cloak (this was no time for niceties), but she jerked away and ran into the house.

Kitty gave an owl cry that was an agreed-upon warning

signal. "Julien and Mélanie will manage. We can create a distraction down here."

Kitty was sensible. It wasn't always easy to be sensible.

A carriage rattled down the street and drew up one house over. A footman sprang down to let down the steps. Just as a scream sounded from inside the house. And a thud. If Malcolm was judging correctly, Julien and Mélanie were on the roof one house over.

Kitty darted into the street. Malcolm followed, both of them trying to scan the roofline. The blonde woman ran back into the street yelling "Bertie!" Her cloak had fallen back, revealing a filmy silver-spangled white gown.

Two ladies whom the footmen had just handed down from the carriage froze, staring at the scene. A young couple—perhaps a footman and housemaid on an evening out—had gone still by the area railings. Nothing like scandal to disturb the quiet of the night.

"Here, now." A man in a dark coat, who looked like a watchman, hurtled into the street and ran up to the blonde woman. "What is this, madam?"

"He's run off." The blonde woman tugged her cloak closed over her gown.

"Who has?" the watchman asked, as two other men ran up behind him and paused, looking to him as their leader. The rest of the watch, no doubt.

"Mr. Caulfield-West. They said he was in the country." The blonde woman waved a hand towards Kitty and Malcolm. "But I saw him. He jumped out the window. With a lady. If you can call her that."

"Mr. Caulfield-West isn't here." The young man who might be a footman ran into the street. "Drove off to the country yesterday with Lambton. His valet. I saw them leave. Lambton said they'd be gone a fortnight at the least."

"You think I don't know what it means when he says he's

going to the country?" The blonde woman pulled her hood over her hair, holding her cloak closed with her other hand. "But I tell you, he didn't this time. He jumped out of the window."

"Wouldn't he have hit the ground then?" The young woman with the footman ran over to join them, the lamplight catching the coppery strands in the dark curls escaping her bonnet.

"Perhaps it was a housebreaker." One of the ladies who had descended from the carriage gasped and clutched her friend's arm. "Good heavens, are we safe going home?" She glanced towards the carriage and then towards the house that appeared to be her own.

The watchman lifted his lantern and swung it in an arc, with the air of a man suddenly realizing he may be called upon to actually undertake heroic work. He jerked his head at his companions. "Fan out. Search the area. Could be an injured man about."

"There." The girl with the coppery hair gestured towards the roof of the building over. "I saw something moving in the shadows."

Damn. Malcolm ran several scenarios through his head. His wife and Julien were well able to take care of themselves. Scrambling up a roof in the midst of the crowd would hardly improve the situation. Still—

A crash sounded from down the street. The blonde woman screamed. "They jumped!"

CHAPTER 3

Raoul O'Roarke leant against the brick wall. Carriage wheels rattled by occasionally. He could hear footsteps, the sound of a chamber pot being dumped by area steps, a young couple whispering goodnight. A far cry from the Spanish mountains or the corridors of a palace. But by god, it felt good to be back in the field. Even if his recent wound still slowed him down enough that he'd had to admit it made no sense for him to be part of the actual break-in. Still, he was glad to offer what assistance he could. Perhaps he was flattering himself that it helped to have someone else in the street, but one never knew when a mission might prove complicated.

Shouts cut the air. From down the street. A medley of voices. Footsteps scrabbled over roof tiles above. Raoul ran down the street. A kestrel call sounded above. He stepped to the side and caught Mélanie as she dropped down from the roof.

"You never miss your mark," he said as he set her on her feet. It was far from the first time he'd caught her in the course of some escape or other. And if his healing wound gave a scream of protest, it was a muffled scream. More a grunt, really.

"Thank you, Raoul." Mélanie touched his arm. "Your wound—"

"Is quite nearly healed. Glad to have been able to help."

"Timely as ever, O'Roarke." Julien dropped down beside Mélanie.

"I shouldn't have needed the help." Mélanie tugged at the string holding up her gown. "But this is harder in a skirt."

"I heard something." The shout came from down the street. "Down that way."

Mélanie's gaze shot to Raoul's and then to Julien's. A career in espionage taught one to communicate without words.

"I think there's only one thing for it," Julien said.

MÉLANIE SMOOTHED her hands over her crumpled skirt. As a playwright, she appreciated a well thought through scene. But there was something to be said for the joys of improvising. Especially with a good improvisational partner. She cast a quick look at Julien. And then at Raoul. Or where Raoul had been. He had melted into the shadows. As he so often did.

Julien took her arm and they stepped forwards. But a crowd was already hurrying towards them.

"That's them," a man shouted. Dark coat, lantern in hand, looked like one of the watch. "I saw them. Jumped off the roof."

"Bertie!" A woman ran forwards, blonde hair and dark cloak streaming behind her. She cast herself on Julien, then drew back and looked at him in confusion.

"I'm desolated to inform you that my name is not Bertie, madam," Julien said. "By whom I suspect you mean Mr. Bertram Caulfield-West."

"You know Bertie?" the woman asked.

Julien tugged his neckcloth smooth. "We were at school together."

"Here, now." The man who appeared to be one of the watch took a step forwards. "Were you in Mr. Caulfield-West's rooms?"

Julien flicked a speck of lint from his sleeve. "Of course I was. Caulfield-West told me to make use of them."

"You jumped out the window," the blonde woman said.

"I should think we did." Julien's voice rang with affront. "Someone broke into the room screaming. We feared for our lives."

"I thought you were Bertie," the blonde woman said, as though that explained everything.

"We?" The watchman glanced round.

Julien coughed. "Slip of the tongue."

"There was a woman with him." The blonde woman's gaze shot to Mélanie.

"This lady and I had availed ourselves of Caulfield-West's rooms to—converse." Julien shifted his weight from one foot to the other. "Naturally we were startled by the intrusion. It could have been thieves."

"A lady alone?" one of the watch said.

"We didn't take time to see how many people there were." Mélanie moved to stand close to Julien.

"A likely story," the blonde woman said.

"What was your business with Mr. Caulfield-West, madam?" the watchman asked.

The blonde woman drew a breath. "Bertie and I—"

"Arthur!" Kitty ran out of the crowd and flung herself on Julien, gripping the lapels of his coat in her fists. "I knew it. I knew you were with her."

"Who are you?" the watchman demanded.

"His wife." Kitty tightened her grip and shook Julien, tawny ringlets falling round her face,

"You said you were married to *him*." The blonde woman

looked round the chaotic group. Her gaze settled on Malcolm. "Him, the tall one."

"Well, of course I did." Kitty looked at the blonde woman, still holding tight to Julien. "We were trying to avoid a scandal. That's the whole reason we came here."

"You tried to stop me from going into Bertie's rooms," the blonde woman said.

"How could I have done otherwise?" Kitty turned to face the blonde woman, gripping Julien's arm as though to anchor him to the ground. "I was watching Arthur. I was determined to catch them. I didn't want you messing the whole thing up."

"My dear Catherine," Julien said, "let me assure you—"

"Don't 'my dear' me." Kitty shot a look at Julien, then turned to Malcolm. "You see, I told you they were together."

"I didn't want to believe it." Malcolm took a step forwards. His gaze fastened on Mélanie, filled with reproach. The sort of reproach he'd never have let her see in real life. "Susan, how could you?"

"Arthur and I only stopped to take shelter on our way back from the theatre," Mélanie said. "If you'd been willing to escort me to the Haymarket tonight none of this would have happened. But you insisted on staying home." She looked from Malcolm to Kitty. "What are you doing here with *her*?"

"I should think that's obvious," Kitty said. "We were both wondering where our spouses were."

"So you were out in the street alone? I mean alone together?"

"How dare you," Kitty said. "Susie, you have no right—"

"Susan. Catherine," Malcolm said. "We're in public."

"I'm not the one who made it public," Kitty said. "I'll never forgive Bertie Caulfield-West."

The secret to improvisation was playing off what one had been given. The crowd was silent round them, riveted by the scene. The longer it went on, the more they'd forget how the night had begun. Mélanie rounded on Kitty. "You always liked Bertie yourself."

"I didn't!" Kitty's denial had just the right note of falseness. "That is, of course I was polite to him, he went to school with my husband, but I never—"

"Don't," Julien said. "Of course you did. You're always flirting with him across the dinner table."

"Don't you dare try to turn the tables, Arthur. I only put up with him because he's your friend. And I know perfectly well what he's up to in the country now, and with whom."

"Oh for that matter so do I." Mélanie tossed her head and felt innumerable strands of hair slither from their pins. "I mean, we all know what he gets up to when he says he's off to visit his friend Bunnington."

"Who's Bunnington?" the blonde woman demanded.

"Caulfield-West's friend," Julien said in repressive tones.

Kitty snorted. "Convenient friend. Whom we've never met."

"Just because you haven't met him—" Julien said.

"Have you met him?"

"Er—"

"Don't tell more lies, Arthur." Kitty rounded on Malcolm. "Have you met him?"

"I'm sure I have." Malcolm coughed.

"Where?"

"Can't quite place it."

"Precisely," Mélanie said. "Whenever Bertie Caulfield-West wants to avoid going to his aunt's dinner party or squiring one of his cousins—"

"Or is worried about a jealous husband," Kitty said.

"—his good friend Bunnington is taken ill. And Mr. Caulfield-West has to go haring off to the country. Only if anyone followed him they'd find him holed up in a cozy inn or someone's hunting box with a pretty maid or a fresh-faced country girl."

"It's not that this time," Kitty said. "I'm quite sure he's with the fair frailty."

"Oh no!" Mélanie said. "Really? I thought that ended ages ago. I was sure he was with her sister."

"Whose sister?" the blonde woman demanded. "Who is he with?"

Mélanie turned to her with a sympathy that was quite genuine. Bertie Caulfield-West had clearly put this woman through a great deal. "If you haven't even heard of Bunnington, you can't know Bertie very well."

"Bertie?" the blonde woman said. "You call him Bertie?"

"We grew up together."

"We all did," Kitty said. "That's part of the problem."

"Bertie never had the least sense," Mélanie said.

Kitty shot a look at her that cut through the shadows. "You almost married him."

"I never! I just—one is so foolish at twenty."

"Only at twenty?" Malcolm muttered.

"I heard that," Mélanie said.

"You're in no position to complain," Malcolm shot back.

"Here, now." The watchman looked round. "Where's the other gentleman got to?"

"What gentleman?" Kitty asked.

"The one we saw down the street. The one who helped this lady"—he gestured to Mélanie—"down from the roof."

"Oh, him." Mélanie tossed her head back, dislodging yet more hair. "We'd never seen him before. He just happened to come by at an opportune moment. I daresay he's gone off about whatever he was doing tonight. I don't think I'd recognize him if I saw him again."

"Do you mean to say you jumped off the roof into some strange man's arms?" Malcolm demanded.

"Of course not," Mélanie said. "I jumped off the roof because I needed to get to the ground. Fortunately this kind gentleman happened to be passing by and caught me, or I'm quite sure I'd have turned an ankle. You should be thanking him."

"You should never have got yourself in this situation in the first place." Malcolm gripped Mélanie's arm. "We should get home and take no more of these kind people's time. Catherine, may we escort you?"

"Thank you." Kitty tightened her grip on Julien's arm. "But I'll go with Arthur. To make sure he gets home."

CHAPTER 4

Mélanie dropped down on the sofa in the library of the house in Berkeley Square that had been Malcolm's and that she now finally thought of as her own. "I forgot how fun it is to improvise."

"The Bunnington addition was genius." Julien leant back on the settee and accepted a glass of whisky from Raoul's wife Laura.

"I met Bertie Caulfield-West once," Kitty said. "He does have a friend named Bunnington. Or claims to. I shouldn't be the least surprised if he's fictional."

"A fictional friend is quite handy for an agent," Mélanie said.

"Yes, but I rather suspect in Mr. Caulfield-West's case the intrigues were more romantic," Kitty said.

Laura set down the whisky decanter. "Where exactly do you think Raoul went?"

"To get the papers, I profoundly hope." Malcolm's voice was easy, but a faint line showed between his eyes. He was never entirely at ease when it came to his father. Especially since Raoul had been wounded.

Mélanie petted Berowne, the family cat, who had jumped up

on her lap. "I must say I'm quite curious to meet Mr. Caulfield-West."

"He sounds fool enough to be in the diplomatic service." Malcolm returned the whisky decanter to the drinks trolley.

"And fools gravitate to other fools." Kitty took a drink of whisky. "Diego Aguilar nearly stopped Argentine independence in its tracks more than once. I suppose it's no wonder he was writing to Caulfield-West."

"And no wonder we had to intercept the papers," Julien said. "Try to intercept the papers." He frowned at his nails. Mélanie shot a look at him. Their failure to retrieve the papers had been niggling at her ever since they jumped through the window.

"No shame in being interrupted." Malcolm perched on the arm of Mélanie's chair. "And it was Kitty and I who couldn't stop Caulfield-West's mistress from interrupting you."

"I keep going over that part," Kitty said. "Wondering if I should have—"

She broke off as the door clicked softly open. They all looked round as Raoul came into the library.

Julien looked across the library at Raoul and said it first. "Tell me you got them."

"Can you doubt it?" Raoul grinned and drew the papers from inside his coat. "Honestly, you couldn't have created a better diversion if we'd set it up. The rooms were unlocked and no one was paying attention. Thank you for giving a wounded retired agent the illusion that adventure was still his."

"Spare us," Malcolm said.

"And stop making me jealous." Laura handed her husband a whisky. Raoul took the whisky in one hand and gave the papers to Kitty with the other.

Kitty flipped through the papers. "Diego never had any discretion. As I was saying. Argentine independence would have proceeded much better without him. And from what we learnt tonight, his friend Bertie Caulfield-West is just as bad. Honestly, one begins to wonder how any country chooses its diplomatic service."

"Bloodlines have a great deal to do with it," Julien said.

"Diego Aguilar is a revolutionary," Kitty pointed out.

"He's still the grandson of a conte."

"Fair enough. But he was a reasonably capable revolutionary, from what I saw during our days in the Argentine."

"A bit hot-headed. But yes," Julien conceded. "He had a decent grasp of tactics. I wouldn't have expected him to spill state secrets."

"I met Bertie Caulfield-West once, when he was posted to the Argentine," Kitty said. "We were seated next to each other at a dinner at the British Commercial Rooms. He was actually a rather amusing dinner partner. And he quite definitely had his mind on flirtation. He was also very free with information about the British plans for the Argentine. Which combined with the flirtation made him quite helpful to associate with."

Julien reached for his whisky. "I didn't know it had gone so far."

"Oh, it didn't go as far as all that." Kitty smiled at her husband. "I didn't need to go that far."

"No need to pry," Julien said.

"Darling. I'd admit it if I had." Kitty frowned. "He actually struck me as cleverer than Diego in a number of ways. But I will confess he seemed rather more concerned with saying something witty than with what the consequences might be of his speech. So perhaps it's not a surprise that he and Diego made so free with comments about Mary Carstairs. Who is apparently Mr. Caulfield-West's cousin. And honestly, the news that an Argentine attaché was the lover of the wife of a senior British diplomat could certainly ruin any hope of the new Argentine government's being recognized by Britain."

"But somehow one's own allies always seem to number the

largest number of idiots rather than the opposition," Malcolm said.

"Trust me, as someone who has played practically every side there is, idiots are everywhere," Julien said.

Kitty turned a paper over. "These would definitely end a marriage and also more than one treaty. Unofficial treaty. And any hope the Argentine have of support from Britain. That's why Luisa was so concerned when she learnt Diego had written to Mr. Caulfield-West. That and the fact that he'd been discussing a shipment of silver sent to pay for guns."

It was hardly a secret that the British were funneling weapons to the Argentine rebels. But officially, Britain's treaty with Spain forbade the British government from aiding the rebels against Spain's colonial power. A power that was already more or less a thing of the past on the ground. Still mentions in official papers could ripple in all sorts of directions.

Kitty's brows drew together. "But there seems to be a page missing."

"Perhaps Mr. Caulfield-West burnt it," Laura said.

"Hard to believe he had the sense to burn one page but not the others," Kitty said, scanning the pages again, fingers taut on the paper.

"What?" Malcolm asked.

"Nothing, perhaps. But given what's in these papers, if someone had access to the papers and stole something else but left this, one rather wonders how serious the information was in the stolen papers."

"What else might Diego have known?" Mélanie stroked Berowne under the chin as he rolled over on her lap. "Did Luisa give you any idea?"

"No." Kitty's fingers trembled on the papers. "Not precisely. Luisa was always very pragmatic about her husband. I don't think there was any other way to stay sane, married to Diego. We got to be good friends. At a time when I badly needed a friend. I trusted her. I do trust her. But she was more than usually concerned about these papers. I can't but think—"

Kitty broke off at a pounding on the door from the hall. Tension shot through the group. Late night arrivals were far from unusual in Berkeley Square. But they usually involved some mission or other. And this came close on the night's adventure. Malcolm exchanged a quick look with Mélanie and went into the hall. Mélanie followed, the others crowding behind, so they all saw as Malcolm opened the door. To find Harry and Cordelia Davenport on the doorstep, and Désirée Clairineau and Tony Bamford just behind them.

"This is a pleasant surprise," Malcolm said, stepping aside to allow the new arrivals into the house. "Is anything wrong?"

"You tell us," Cordelia said, the hood of her cloak falling back from her blonde ringlets. "We all got your note, and we all met on the doorstep. Only we're quite sure the note was forged."

"What did it say?" Malcolm asked.

Cordelia and Désirée each held out a paper. Mélanie moved closer to her husband to read it. The writing was practically identical.

Come to Berkeley Square at once. Dire emergency.
Rannoch

"It's not a bad forgery," Malcolm said. "But I'd never say 'dire emergency.'"

"Or sign yourself 'Rannoch.'" Harry pulled off his hat.

Tony Bamford's gaze swept the group in the hall. "It looks as though some of you have had an adventure tonight."

"Yes." Mélanie smoothed her hands over her sarcenet skirt, pressing down the torn bits. Which Berowne might have made worse. "But we're quite all right now. At least, we wouldn't call it a dire emergency. You'd best come into the library and we can sort this out. What on earth—"

Another rap sounded on the door before any of them had taken more than half a step towards the library.

Alarm spread through the company again. Someone clearly had some reason for wanting them all gathered together.

Malcolm opened the door. This time to see his cousin Judith and her husband Jeremy Roth. And the couple who were the talk of Mayfair—Jeremy's sister Harriet and her betrothed, the composer and noted roué Tristram Gresham.

"You see." Judith kissed Malcolm's cheek and swept past him into the hall. "I told you it was a set up, darling." She looked back over her shoulder at Jeremy, then turned back to Malcolm and Mélanie. "Thank goodness you're all all right." She glanced round the company assembled in the hall. "You *are* all right, aren't you?"

"More or less," Mélanie said.

Judith ran her gaze over Mélanie's tattered black sarcenet gown, then glanced at Julien, whose pantaloons had a torn knee and whose neckcloth and collar were decidedly grimy. Not to mention that he was missing a button from his coat and two from his waistcoat. "You look as though you've come from an adventure. I don't know whether to be concerned or envious. But don't worry, I won't pry. That's one thing I've learnt in the first months of our marriage."

Jeremy snorted as he, Harriet, and Gresham followed Judith into the hall. "It was fairly obvious the note was a forgery."

"The question is whose?" Gresham said.

"And why?" Harriet looked round the group. "I mean, someone obviously wanted to gather us all together. But to what end?"

Julien glanced round the hall, gaze lingering on the fanlight over the door. "Uncle Hubert once had someone shoot a rifle into this house."

"I forgot you were here for that," Malcolm said.

"Well, not when the rifle shots actually went off. But I was trying to fix things. The whole situation was all rather my fault."

"It was much more Hubert's," Malcolm said.

"That seems a bit extreme even for Hubert," Désirée said. "I trust he had his reasons?"

"He was more than usually desperate," Malcolm said. "Though at the time I was convinced I'd never forgive him. And I'd certainly never have believed I'd let him across our doorstep again."

"Hubert tends to bring out that reaction in people," Kitty said.

Judith glanced round the hall. "Where's Julien? He was here just a moment ago."

"Probably doing a perimeter check," Mélanie said. "Back to the old days. He never used to arrive at our house or leave it by the front door, and he had a habit of disappearing into the shadows."

"He did the same in the Argentine," Kitty said. "Often at inopportune moments. I never quite mastered the trick. Or got used to his habit of disappearing and reappearing. A year and a half of marriage and he still takes me by surprise."

They moved back into the library, and Malcolm and Laura set about pouring more whisky.

A few minutes later, Julien returned. Or more accurately materialized. Mélanie thought he'd come through a window, though she couldn't be entirely sure. Even watching for it, it was hard to tell where he came from.

Julien strolled over to the group by the fireplace. "I don't see anyone outside. This seems a bit excessive as a way to attack us, but better to be safe."

Another rap sounded on the door as the last whisky glass was passed round. Mélanie exchanged a look with Malcolm. Who was missing? Possibly Malcolm's aunt Frances and her husband, Harry's uncle Archie. Or Bertrand Laclos and Rupert Caruthers?

Of one accord they moved back into the hall, the others crowding behind. Malcolm eased the door open, more slowly than the last time.

To find John Southcott on the doorstep, regarding him with a level gaze. Much the same gaze he'd worn at their last encounter in Berkeley Square, when they'd accused him of murder.

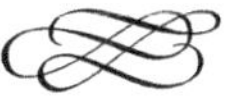

"Southcott." Malcolm opened the door wider. "This is a surprise."

"Good evening, Rannoch. My apologies for calling late."

Malcolm cast a quick glance over his shoulder at Mélanie. She inclined her head. Southcott was a threat—they knew he'd been behind at least one murder. But it was difficult to imagine what damage he could do personally in the house—any of them were a match for him—and all things considered better to hear what he had to say. And why he was determined to say it now.

"You'd best come in." Malcolm stepped to the side, gaze trained on Southcott.

"Mr. Southcott," Mélanie said, as Southcott stepped into the hall. "We weren't expecting you tonight. Though I think perhaps we should have been."

"Mrs. Rannoch." Southcott inclined his head a very correct half inch. "My apologies for the late hour. And you seem to be entertaining." His gaze swept the group.

"Yes, it's a somewhat impromptu party," Mélanie said in a bright voice. "We're delighted to see our friends. I think perhaps we have you to thank for their arrival?"

"I can't imagine why you'd think that." Southcott removed his hat from his close-cropped dark hair and glanced round as though looking for a footman to hand it to.

"Can't you? We could pull out the notes and check them against your handwriting. But why don't you come into the library and tell us about it instead?"

Southcott met her gaze for a moment. He was a man who thought everything through. Mélanie could see the calculation behind his gaze. Attempt to continue with the facade of normal social interaction or give in and admit his schemes. He was not a man who dropped his mask easily. After a long moment, he inclined his head and followed her into the library. One had to give him credit for persistence. How many could keep up a pose of normalcy about a call at this hour of the night?

He hesitated just inside the library door, meeting Tony's gaze. "Uncle Tony."

"John." Tony inclined his head a precise quarter of an inch.

Southcott's gaze moved over Tony's shoulder. "Mademoiselle Clairineau."

"Don't say you're surprised to see us, Mr. Southcott," Désirée said. "You have too much wit to pretend that's the case and surely you believe we have too much wit to believe it."

Southcott coughed. He glanced away, then went still as he met Harriet's gaze.

"Good evening, John." Harriet's voice and gaze were steady, though she was gripping Tristram's hand tightly. Tristram's gaze was fixed on a point across the room as though secrets of immense interest lay hidden in the library cornice.

Berowne ran to Mélanie's skirts, gaze fixed on Southcott. Mélanie scooped him up, returned to her chair, and waved Southcott to a straight-backed chair across the room. "Do sit down, Mr. Southcott." She patted Berowne, who was regarding Southcott through slitted eyes. "You have the floor. I presume you didn't go to such lengths to bring us all here without a plan for how you were going to proceed once we were assembled."

Southcott seated himself, flicking back the tails of his coat. A rapid series of calculations seemed to occur behind his gaze. "You're quite right, of course, Mrs. Rannoch. This is not an accidental gathering. My apologies for the rather unorthodox invitations—"

"Invitations?" Harriet said.

Southcott cast a quick glance at her, then looked round the room. "I knew none of you would accept a conventional invitation. I realize the hour is late, but I did not wish to delay speaking to you. It seemed imperative to have this discussion soon. For all our sakes."

"I suppose that's supposed to sound intriguing?" Kitty said.

"You needn't listen, of course, Lady Carfax." Southcott met her gaze. "But I can say with conviction that it would be in your interest to do so."

"This isn't a diplomatic paper, Southcott." Julien leant back on the arm of Kitty's chair, at once relaxed and coiled to spring. Like a panther. "You needn't go on for paragraphs before you come to the point."

Southcott settled back in his chair, head held high, hands on his thighs. Drawing out the moment for advantage? Or pulling his thoughts together? He had formidable skills, as they had seen. But he was new to this. That could give them an advantage. His gaze swept the group. "It's been some time since we've spoken. I trust you are well. In the circumstances, I did not think we would easily find a time to speak at conventional social events. Certainly not all of us together. I did think of trying to speak to you at the opening of Gresham's opera—"

"Good lord," Tristram said. "You amaze me, Southcott. I shouldn't have thought you'd be in the least interested. Or that you even knew about it, for that matter."

Southcott met Tristram's gaze, his own as cool and steady as the Serpentine on a windless winter day. "One can have many reasons for attending the opera, Gresham. As I'm sure even someone absorbed with his own compositions would realize. Anyone interested in the doings of London society would wish to be there. And I believe the king means to be present."

"Ah," Harriet said, "of course. You would wish to be present in that case."

Southcott met her gaze for a moment. "In any event," he said, as though he were speaking of organizing a dinner party, "given the amount of activity that night, it hardly seemed prudent or even feasible to gather everyone together. And I think you will appreciate the efficiency of doing this all at once—"

"Efficiency, Southcott," Julien said.

"I realize the hour is late," Southcott continued in repressive tones, without acknowledging the interruption. "But other circumstances made me think I could find a number of you already gathered in Berkeley Square tonight."

"A number of us live here," Raoul said. With no sign that he recognized the risks in Southcott's knowing of tonight's mission.

Southcott's gaze swept the group. For all his stodgy manner, that gaze could send chills. He'd made it clear he was not one to trifle with. "Just so. And I had reason to believe the Carfaxes would be here as well."

"Oh, that name," Julien said.

"At this hour I felt I could count on finding the rest of you at home, where you would promptly respond to messages from friends," Southcott continued. "My apologies for the deception. But I did not think you would respond to an invitation in my own name."

"We might have done," Harry said. "We'd have been curious. We are curious."

"Mr. Southcott." Cordelia put a hand on her husband's arm. "Why did you wish to speak with all of us?"

Southcott drew in and released his breath. "You all made some quite fanciful statements about me when last we met. I realize tempers were running high, and I hope we can all now accept those words for the fantasy they are. I do understand that we have some very talented fiction writers in this group." His gaze moved from Mélanie to Laura. "However, I feel compelled to say that should you ever choose to share these stories with others—even as speculation—there are things I would feel compelled to share in return."

The unease that had been coiling through Mélanie tightened. She felt an alarm shoot through Malcolm. She put a hand on his arm. No sense in revealing anything until they knew what Southcott knew.

John Southcott's gaze fastened on Mélanie. "You know my association with Frederick Radley, Mrs. Rannoch. He has shared some stories with me. Stories of his past association with you in the Peninsula. He says he shared them with Rannoch as well. I am too much of a gentleman to repeat those stories in front of others—to repeat them at all."

"That rather prevents your doing anything with them." Mélanie tightened her fingers on Malcolm's arm. They had already known Southcott was allied with Radley. They'd assumed Radley had shared his past association with Mélanie with Southcott. This merely confirmed what they had already suspected. But Malcolm, though generally a very sensible man, was inclined to go into protective panic at any indication her past might come to light.

"I hope never to have to do anything with this information," Southcott said. "But should I find myself threatened, I'd feel compelled to remove the gloves."

"Meaning you're only a gentleman when you find it convenient." Julien folded his arms over his chest.

Southcott sent a quite wasted quelling glance in Julien's direction and then turned his gaze to Malcolm. "I trust you wish your wife's secrets to remain secret, Rannoch. But should you need further incentive, allow me to point out that war office ledgers hold a number of secrets of their own. Without examining those ledgers, I doubt I'd ever have guessed your brother was an agent."

Malcolm's arm muscles tightened beneath Mélanie's hand. But he kept his gaze steady and didn't respond to Southcott with so much as a flicker of an eyelid.

Southcott watched him for the length of a heartbeat, waiting for a reaction he didn't get. "I know Hubert Mallinson was paying Edgar Rannoch. I'm quite sure Edgar was playing both sides. I'm also quite sure I know who killed him." His gaze shifted to Julien. "I'm not entirely sure why. But I have my suspicions."

Julien's fingers had gone taut on Kitty's shoulder. His gaze too was steady. But perhaps had never been more lethal. "Lots of people have suspicious, Southcott."

"So they do. But some are more accurate than others. As I said, I have a sense of what you were all doing tonight. And what it might concern."

"That's a rather vague statement, Southcott." Julien's voice was cool as a steel blade.

Southcott met the gaze of one of the Continent's most dangerous assassins—former assassins—without flinching. "Would you prefer me to elaborate? I thought not." Southcott looked from Raoul to Tony. "Of course, nothing quite reaches the level of the secrets the two of you have been hiding in official ledgers for decades. Keeping a French agent in the employ of the foreign office."

Tony leant back on the settee, legs crossed at the ankle. "I know you aren't a field agent, John," he said in a bored voice, "but surely you've heard of double agents."

"Is that what you call someone in the pay of Britain but selling secrets to the French?"

"Secrets can go multiple ways, John."

"Somehow I don't think Mademoiselle Clairineau would have colluded with you in duping France."

"Perhaps Tony was duping me," Désirée said. "He did get the better of me. On occasion."

"Rare occasions." Tony reached for her hand.

"With all due respect, Uncle Tony, I doubt you pulled the wool over Mademoiselle Clairineau's and O'Roarke's very astute gazes. The three of you were playing both sides. Of course, you aren't the only ones with secrets." Southcott's gaze moved to Kitty. "Your work in the Argentine was even more complicated than it appeared at first glance. When Carfax sent you there, I doubt he intended for you to collude with revolutionaries. And then there's the question of why you were so eager to leave the Peninsula in the first place. Which I can't help but think is connected to my suspicions about your current husband."

Kitty didn't move a muscle. Her ruby earrings didn't so much as shimmer in the candlelight. Julien looked as though he were coiled for attack. And Mélanie felt the tension tighten in Malcolm's arm. "Your mind appears to make quite dizzying leaps of imagination, Mr. Southcott," Kitty said. "Perhaps you're the one who should consider a career in fiction."

"I fear I am quite lacking in imagination, Lady Carfax. I couldn't possibly invent anything half so interesting as the truths that lie hidden in public records. Such as Lord Gresham's activities in Naples."

"Which activities?" Gresham was seemingly relaxed in a corner of the sofa, his shoulder brushing Harriet's. "I freely admit to a number of activities in Naples, as well as just about every other city I've visited. Though I would like to protect others involved, for myself I have no worries about anything that might come to light."

Something tightened in the back of Southcott's eyes. He was

a master of control, but even he had his weak points. Good to know. "Your romantic adventures are your own business, Gresham. And Miss Roth's now. But we both know you are far more than the idle fribble you appear—"

"My dear Southcott. May I quote you on that?"

"—and you were engaged in a number of other activities in Naples. Which I think you would prefer not to have come to light for the sake of those involved and of the cause you seem to love so well, however misguided it may be."

"You could say as much based on public knowledge of my life."

"But I wouldn't know to mention a certain night at the Palazzo Reale."

Gresham went still, though his gaze remained steady. "That doesn't prove anything."

"No. But to a man of your understanding surely it suggests a great deal."

"One may read suggestion a number of ways, Southcott."

"And I credit you with being too sensible a man to ignore it." Southcott's gaze moved to Roth. "You run a remarkable number of risks, Mr. Roth. For a man whose work is to uphold the law, you are certainly willing to bend it. To put the most charitable construction possible on it."

"Tell me you haven't done the same, Mr. Southcott." Jeremy's fingers had curled inwards but his voice was steady. He was perhaps more experienced than any of them at facing down men like Southcott. And he made it a point of pride not to give way to the powerful. Though whether or not the word applied to Southcott was a matter of debate.

"Not nearly as often and not nearly so recklessly. I don't have anything like your daring, Roth."

"On the contrary, Southcott. I believe daring is one thing no one can deny you possess. In spades."

"I prefer to think of it as strategic risk. I understand your loyalties, Roth, but I'm not sure how strategic it was to have taken actions that Sir Nathaniel and Lord Sidmouth would both surely abhor. Of course, perhaps you're no longer concerned with your career and what your superiors at Bow Street may think. I'm sure you could live quite comfortably on your wife's fortune."

Jeremy's shoulders tightened. For an instant, Mélanie thought he was going to push himself out of his chair. He released his breath. "A crude blow, Southcott. I expected something more sophisticated from you."

"Sometimes the most direct blow is the most effective. Of course, Lady—that is, Mrs. —Roth's secrets are more complicated. I'm not even sure I understand all of them. But as a devoted mother, I'm sure Mrs. Roth wouldn't wish her late husband's activities to reach her daughter's ears."

"Serena hasn't the least interest in her late father's activities, Mr. Southcott," Judith said. "She's was little more than a baby when he died."

"But children have a way of growing up. And if my comments to Mr. Roth seemed crude, perhaps it will be subtler when I say that I don't think either of you would wish your children to know of their late parents' activities."

"By god, John." It was Tony's voice that cut through the room. "I underestimated you. Until now I thought there were some depths to which you wouldn't sink."

Southcott met his uncle's gaze, steel clashing against steel. "When threatened, we all have to use whatever means at hand to defend ourselves. I'm sure your fiancée would agree. I'm sure she's resorted to a number of methods that cost her sleep. Or perhaps I do her too much credit in thinking so."

"It's an interesting question," Désirée said. "Of course, we can never know what we might be capable of in the right circumstances. And I freely admit I've been willing to cross any number of lines. But the thing is, I've never been so thoroughly put in check as to see what I'd do in the circumstances you now face."

Southcott's face flushed pink. And then red.

Désirée sat back in her chair.

Tony regarded her like Antony watching Cleopatra in her barge. "A palpable hit."

"It's all very well." Southcott's face was still red, but he'd recovered his voice. "You can congratulate yourself on winning a volley. But this is a long match. And what you all need to realize is that I have the power to win it. And I'm not afraid to use that power. If I'm pushed hard enough."

"You haven't threatened me with anything," Harriet said, her fingers twined tightly with Gresham's.

"And I don't intend to." Southcott met her gaze, his own steady. "Whatever Uncle Tony says, we all have lines we won't cross."

Harriet returned his gaze. "I wouldn't have expected that to be yours."

"Wouldn't you?" Southcott gave a faint smile. "But then there are a number of things we didn't understand about each other, I believe. I think my concern for you is apparent. You've made some dangerous choices." His gaze flickered to Gresham. "I have no wish to add to your challenges."

Southcott drew a quick breath, as though aware he was on treacherous ground. "Of course, the courtesy doesn't extend to your brother. Mr. Roth has made some interesting decisions in the course of his work at Bow Street. I imagine all it would take is a few words in Sir Nathaniel's and Lord Sidmouth's ears to point them to what they should be looking at."

"They might have their own reasons for ignoring it," Gresham said.

"Perhaps. But it's difficult to ignore something when it's explicitly called to one's attention. And then there's the charming Mrs. O'Roarke." Southcott looked at Laura. "You seem to have a knack for staying in the background. But Miss Roth isn't the only one with correspondents abroad. I know quite a few details about your time in India and your first marriage. And more particularly about your relationship with your late father-in-law, the Duke of Trenchard. People do love a scandal, as Gresham mentioned. But while Gresham may not care what is said about him, I can't imagine this is a scandal you would wish to have shared. Even as rumor."

Laura's face was a model of composure. "I never listen to rumors, Mr. Southcott."

"Even when they could impact your daughter?"

"You're vile, John," Harriet said. "But then you just showed that with Jeremy and Judith. And everyone else."

"On the contrary." Southcott met Harriet's gaze. "I share the unvarnished truth. Isn't that what you pride yourself on doing?"

"Not when all it does is hurt people."

"Information is currency," Southcott said. "Surely all the spies in this room understand that. I'm using currency to stake out a position. That's all. We all have ends we wish to achieve. We all have ways we go about achieving them. You can hardly say I'm the only person in this room capable of ruthless tactics. In fact, I'd say I'm something of a novice compared to most of you." His gaze moved to Cordelia. "Radley also has some interesting details to share about your entanglement with Lord Thurston."

"That's ancient history," Cordelia said in a steady voice. "And far less interesting than the more ancient history my husband and I study. Less salacious as well. The Julio-Claudians are difficult to compete with when it comes to scandal."

"That would rather depend on the reader, I think," Southcott said. "Degrees of scandal are open to interpretation. Thurston wrote to Radley. About his friendship with you. It never fails to surprise me how shockingly indiscreet people can be when they put pen to paper. I think you all know the risks that can lie in the written word."

Cordelia's hand shot to Harry's wrist. Before Harry could push himself out of his chair. "My dear Mr. Southcott. I don't know what you imagine I'm afraid of. I've been a social outcast. I've been given the cut direct. I'll admit there are times I enjoy that we now have something of a position back in society. But it would hardly cause me to lose sleep if I lost my vouchers to Almack's and wasn't invited anywhere but into the homes of the people present in this room. I've smiled down whispers. I've ignored slights. I can do it again. And I imagine my husband would be quite delighted if our social circle were limited."

"Quite." Harry smiled, though his shoulders were taut and his gaze lethal.

Southcott's gaze was steady as a steel blade under the onslaught of attacks from round the room. "Your daughters may feel differently when they grow up."

"Livia and Drusilla will find people who appreciate them," Cordelia said. "And they'll understand where true worth lies."

"You have a great deal of fortitude, Lady Cordelia. But it's one thing to talk about defying scandal. It's another to actually go through the repercussions of scandal."

"You forget, Mr. Southcott." Cordelia said, in a gentle voice she might have used with her daughters. "I've been through it. The threat of having scandalous secrets revealed rings a bit hollow when one's scandalous secrets have been common knowledge for nearly a decade."

Southcott's brows twitched together. He was ready to parry threat with the clash of a new threat. He wasn't prepared for someone who let her guard down entirely. He drew a breath and shifted his gaze to Harry. "Of course, there's the issue of your uncle."

Mélanie could imagine the flash of horror that ran through Harry, but he gave no betraying sign of it. "Like Cordelia, I imagine my uncle would have little concern about past scandals being brought to light. Being a man, he'd be the first to say he could stare them down more easily and that they could even add lustre to his name. And he'd be the first to point out the unfairness of that. But regardless, he's happy with the life he has now and would be supremely unconcerned with any rumors that might impact society."

"Admirable. Your uncle's domestic bliss with Lady Frances is quite remarkable. But those aren't the rumors I was thinking of." Southcott settled back in his chair, with the air of a barrister ready to make his closing remarks. "The secrets hidden in official account books can be difficult to decipher. But I've deduced a fair amount about Archibald Davenport. Difficult to see how others didn't arrive at it sooner. But then the lack of attention paid to data hiding in plain sight by those in the foreign office, and war office, and home office, and just about any government office has always been one of my chief complaints about our government. They wasted a lot of money running elaborate missions abroad when they might have just paid attention to what was in their own ledgers."

"I suspect that was directed at me," Tony said. "I might remind you I funded the majority of my own operations abroad. Certainly the more extravagant parts of them."

"I can vouch for that," Désirée said. "Your uncle would never have trusted the foreign office to fill the wine cellar in his safe cottage."

"I didn't come here to quibble about vintners' bills," Southcott said. "I have no doubt that all of you have been extravagant, both with the purse of the British crown and on your own account. The pertinent detail in this case remains. Official ledgers offer clues to a very interesting story about Archibald Davenport's past activities. And yours, O'Roarke. You're all very adept at dismissing scandal. But I imagine even you would pause at an outright accusation of treason."

The word settled over the room. The word that had haunted Mélanie's life and marriage from the moment Malcolm had learnt the truth of her past. Berowne dug his claws into Mélanie's leg. Mélanie couldn't blame him.

"I don't see that anyone has mentioned treason," Cordelia said in a bright voice.

"Not yet, perhaps," Southcott returned in an easy tone. "Because there hasn't been any need to do so. Your husband might say his uncle's activities are in the past. I can see that argument. In my opinion we waste too much time re-fighting the battles of the last half century instead of keeping an eye on the future. I don't necessarily see the need to drag Archibald Davenport's past into the light." He hesitated a moment, savoring his power. "At least, not unless explicitly called upon to do so."

"I don't see that anyone is calling upon you to do anything, Southcott," Julien said.

"We all defend our own, Lord Carfax," Southcott said. "I'm sure you see that better than anyone."

"So I do. The question is what you have to defend that matters so much to you."

"I should have thought that was obvious," Southcott said. "England."

CHAPTER 6

*S*ilence settled over the library as the door clicked shut behind John Southcott. Mélanie had felt similar silences after a skirmish. Or a full-blown battle. One could almost smell the tang of gunsmoke and see gray puffs drifting in the air. She sank her fingers into Berowne's soft fur, anchoring herself.

"Well," Julien said. "That was interesting."

"You have a genius for understatement." Malcolm pushed himself to his feet and moved to the drinks trolley.

"We all need to have a genius for something." Julien looked round the room.

"He's managed to gather an extraordinary amount of information," Laura said.

Kitty nodded. "Difficult to know how many details he knows and how much he's reaching with his suspicions. But even those suspicions—"

Julien put a hand over her own. Kitty gripped his fingers.

The weight of Southcott's implied threats settled over the room, tightening chests and forcing air from lungs.

Kitty drew a breath, as though struggling to recover her

voice. "He knew where we'd been tonight. Or at least that we'd been on a mission. I suspect he knew where. Which makes me wonder if Southcott is the one who took those missing pages in Caulfield-West's papers. The ones I said must be more dangerous than the distinctly dangerous secrets that are already in Diego's letters." She hesitated, fingers white round Julien's own.

"Kitkat—" Julien said.

"They're our friends, Julien. And we need them. Diego's wife Luisa and I were friends. She was as close as I had to a confidante at a time when I needed a confidante. Before you. I told her things about Leo. Not everything. But if she shared those details with Diego and Diego shared them with Caulfield-West and Southcott has those pages—" Kitty's voice caught for a moment, like fabric tugged taut over jagged rock. "That means he knows a great deal."

Julien folded Kitty's hand between both his own. "No way to be sure of any of it. But we have to assume he knows a great deal." He looked round the library. "This can't be the first time most of us have been the victims of blackmail."

"Some of us probably more than others," Désirée said. She had been sitting quietly, her hands tightly folded. "It's quite tempting to dare a blackmailer to do their worst. Though not always practicable. John's still a novice when it comes to blackmail. And he made some tactical errors. But that doesn't mean he can't be lethal."

"My apologies," Tony said. "For being related to him."

"You can't be said to be responsible for him," Kitty said.

"You're very kind, Kitty. I may not have raised him, but I was there when he was growing up. I should have done better. Spent more time with him."

"That might have sent him even more strongly in the opposite direction, my dear," Désirée said. "He seems determined to be quite the opposite of you and his father."

"And seeing more of us might have made him even more determined to go in the opposite direction of our example?" Tony said. "I fear you may be right. Though Lionel and I are hardly similar. And the idea that knowing either of us better would have pushed him more firmly in the other direction is not a pleasant thought. I'm well served."

"You can set a good example, Tony. You can't control what people will make of it."

"Ah, but that's the question." Tony's tone was light but his eyes were weary. "Did I set a good example?"

"My dear." Désirée reached for his hand. "You're you."

Tony kissed her knuckles. "Charming, my love. And far too romantic and deluded for you."

"I refuse to admit to either. Well, at least not to being deluded."

"He was vile," Judith said. "But he didn't say he'd use any of the information. He just wants our silence. And you aren't planning to expose him. You don't have the evidence to do so, at least according to Jeremy."

"Jeremy's right." Raoul said. "We realized when we confronted Southcott a fortnight ago that we couldn't prove anything and the best we could do is watch him. But the next time Southcott wants something? When it's a political favor? The name of an agent? A vote from Malcolm or Julien or Tony? Or me, if I win the by-election. He has an arsenal of leverage to use against us. Désirée's right. He's still learning finesse. But he's ruthless."

"You have something to hold over him," Judith pointed out.

"But we don't have proof." Malcolm set down the whisky decanter. "And I'm very much afraid Southcott does."

"Radley doesn't know that much," Mélanie said, "all things considered. He's tiresome, but there's a limit to what he could have told Southcott. Even if he put it in writing."

"Not precisely comforting." Malcolm moved back from the drinks trolley with a tray of refilled whisky glasses.

"You and Raoul have pardons," Tony said.

"You know about that?" Malcolm paused, the tray tilting precariously in his hands. The pardons, the work of Malcolm's aunt Frances and her connections to the king, were the only reason Malcolm had felt safe abandoning their self-imposed exile and returning to Britain.

"I've heard it mentioned." Tony's gaze was level and friendly, and his smile more than usually sweet. "Mind you, I have good sources. I shouldn't think it's generally known, even in White-hall. Or understood. There can be many reasons for a pardon. And knowing Raoul, I understood how to put the pieces together as others wouldn't."

"Radley could make things uncomfortable." Mélanie took the whisky tray from Malcolm and set it on the sofa table. "But I don't think even Southcott can properly fit the pieces together." Berowne, dislodged from her lap when she took the tray, settled back down again. "After all, they are quite improbable pieces."

"Archie doesn't have a pardon," Harry said in a low voice.

Mélanie had been deeply aware of the irony from the moment Frances told them of the pardons. She'd been able to arrange the pardons for Mélanie and Raoul based on whispers of their activities abroad. Mélanie was French-Spanish. Raoul was Spanish-Irish. Hubert Mallinson, Britain's unofficial spymaster, knew about their activities. In fact, his knowledge was the reason they'd fled Britain at Malcolm's insistence. Archie was British and an MP without a whisper of scandal against him. Frances couldn't use her influence to seek a pardon for the man she had just married without raising questions about his activities. And yet Archie was in more danger than any of them.

"It's a risk." Tony met Harry's gaze.

"You know about that too?" Harry said.

"O'Roarke didn't tell me, if that's what you mean." Tony chose his words carefully. "I've learnt to read round the edges. I've always liked your uncle."

Harry nodded, mouth tight. "I'm going to do everything I can to protect Archie. Obviously, I can't expect the rest of you to."

"Don't talk rot," Julien said. "We'd none of us let the others down. I think that's what being friends means. Being a bit late to it."

"I got your uncle into this," Raoul said.

Harry met Raoul's gaze. At the time of the United Irish Uprising, Raoul had been a young revolutionary running spy missions. Archie had been an MP appalled at his government's actions abroad. Their alliance had later stretched to France and the Peninsula. "Archie would be the first to say he's responsible for his own actions," Harry said.

"And also the first to help me and any of the rest of us if we needed it," Raoul countered.

Malcolm leant forwards. "Archie's being threatened because of us. That makes it all the more imperative we help. Not that we wouldn't help in any case."

"John learnt to play a far tougher game across the negotiating table than I credited when I saw him at work in Vienna and Paris," Tony said.

"Uncle Hubert would probably say it would be far easier simply to eliminate Southcott." Julien frowned and reached for his whisky. "There was a time I'd have agreed with him. Damned difficult to have developed a conscience."

"He'll have left copies of whatever evidence he has, and instructions to reveal it, if anything happens to him," Kitty said. "Raoul's right that he obviously has things in writing. He's clever enough to have thought we might try to eliminate him, and I doubt he credits us with any sort of conscience. Not apparently having one himself."

"But we need to at least get the originals," Mélanie said. "He's probably got those in his rooms."

"He was a bit too self-satisfied when he left," Désirée said. "He thinks he has us boxed in. I don't think he realizes how used we all are to living with exposure."

"Or how creative we can be," Julien said.

Kitty turned to look at her husband. "Assuming Southcott's hiding things in his lodgings, we need to break in. And make sure he isn't there."

"He's going to the *Liliana* opening," Harriet said. "He made a big point of it. Especially since the king plans to be there."

"Yes, I noted that too." Julien settled back against the chair back, arms folded. "Southcott lodges in St. Albans Place, as I recall. Not so far from the greater Covent Garden and the King's Theatre. Assuming he really is in the theatre for the opera, some of us could slip out during the performance." He glanced at Tristram. "Apologies, Gresham."

"No need." Tristram waved a hand. "Plenty of other times for you to see the full performance."

"We'll have to make sure his servants are out as well," Kitty said.

"We can manage that," Désirée said. "A mission with multiple roles. My favorite."

Mélanie scratched Berowne's ears. "I could—"

Julien shook his head. "You need to remain in place. Southcott's likely to be watching you. Harriet definitely needs to be in place."

"We were going to bring the children," Mélanie. "I suppose—"

"By all means, no," Julien said. "That is, don't change the plans. We'll have ours there as well. More distraction."

"Julien," Kitty said. "You just suggested using our children as distraction on a mission."

"Don't pretend anyone here hasn't done it, sweetheart."

"True," Malcolm said. To Mélanie's relief, he didn't protest. "Though it may not be brazen enough to deceive Southcott."

"Julien and I should be able to handle the break-in," Kitty said. "We can slip out during the performance."

"Laura and I can handle his staff," Raoul said.

"A distraction in the theatre would be good," Cordelia said. "When you're slipping out."

"Nothing like a scandal to cause distraction," Judith said. "Especially at the theatre. Everyone's scanning the boxes for it. More than looking at the stage. Sorry, Tristram."

"It's a fact of life," Gresham said.

"And we happen to have representatives of the most enticing scandal in London right here in this group." Judith looked from Désirée to Tony. "Tony's divorce is still the talk of London. You'll be a distraction just by showing up. Though it would be better if you could create some sort of scene right as the others are slipping out."

"You're a brilliant strategist, Judith," Désirée said. "We can certainly stage a quarrel."

"We can," Tony said. "Though it would be better if it involved someone else."

"Hetty?" Désirée asked on a note of at once surprise and admiration. In the past weeks she'd become friends with Tony's wife, but Hetty hadn't actually been involved in a mission.

"Oh, that's perfect," Judith said.

"I think she'd help," Tony said. "In fact, I think she'd enjoy it. And she won't ask questions. She spent decades as the wife of a diplomat."

"She spent decades as the wife of a spy," Désirée said.

"That too."

"What if John doesn't show up? Or leaves during the opera?" Harriet asked.

"If he doesn't show up, we cancel," Mélanie said. "If he leaves —we'll make sure he doesn't."

"How?" Harriet asked.

"We'll need someone to distract him. And I can see the perfect candidate."

"Oh." Harriet met her gaze.

"If you're willing."

"Of course. But I mean—do you really think he'd want to talk to me?"

"I think he has a great deal he wants to say to you," Mélanie said. "That much was clear tonight."

"And he always underestimates you," Désirée said. "His pride won't let him guess he's being set up. And he won't be able to stop talking. He likes to talk, that one."

"He does indeed," Harriet agreed. She glanced at Tristram.

"Sorry, sweetheart," he said. "But I'll be conducting. And I think I can help best by staying out of Southcott's way."

"I didn't mean that. I can certainly handle John without you. But would you—"

Gresham gave a faint smile. "I trust you, Harriet. How could I do otherwise when you've taken the great leap of trusting me?"

"Silly." Harriet touched her fingers to his face. "Right. I should be able to distract John." She glanced round the group. "Do you think it will work?"

"If it doesn't," Julien said, "we have a few days to think of something else."

CHAPTER 7

*M*alcolm pulled off his coat. "It cuts close to the bone."

"Of course it does." Mélanie undid the strings on her gown. The same black gown that she had worn to break into Bertie Caulfield-West's rooms. The skirt was torn—she was going to have to see what her companion Blanca could do with it, when she and her husband Addison returned from their family visit. That goodness they were away. God knows what Southcott would have threatened them with. It seemed another lifetime when they had dressed for the mission. Which it had been, in a way. John Southcott's threats had shaken their world on end. "We're all family."

"Yes, but Leo—"

Mélanie tugged at a knotted string. "Is your nephew."

"Our nephew." Malcolm set his coat on the back of his favorite frayed green velvet chair. "Not that that makes him any more important to us than the rest of Kitty and Julien's children. I mean, they're all—"

"Of course. And I'm quite sure Kitty and Julien feel the same about Colin and Jessica."

Malcolm nodded. "But with Leo there's no denying—I mean, I can't ignore—"

"You feel responsible."

"If it weren't for me, none of this would have happened."

"You aren't responsible for your brother's crimes."

"Of course not." Malcolm smoothed his coat over the chair back with taut fingers. "But my own actions helped set him on this course."

Even given the mines that lay in their past, this was particularly fraught ground. Because it involved the brother Malcolm had loved, who had betrayed him in multiple ways. And Kitty, who was now their friend and part of their extended family, but who had once been Malcolm's lover. "Edgar set himself on a very distinct course quite on his own."

Malcolm stared down at his hands on the dark superfine. "Edgar set himself on a course opposed to me."

"That was part of it. But not all, I think. You're magnetic, Malcolm. I don't think you realize how much you influence people. Mostly for the better—like Sandy Trenor. Or Ben Smythe. But that magnetism can also provoke jealousy. It's quite obvious Edgar was jealous of you for countless reasons—"

"Including the fact that I was the heir, but he was the only one of us who was Alistair Rannoch's son."

"I think, more than that, it's that he sensed Alistair wished you were his son rather than Edgar. But you didn't drive everything about Edgar."

"No." Malcolm flushed. "Of course not. But if Kit and I hadn't—"

"Don't you dare, Malcolm." Mélanie took a step forwards, her gown slipping from her shoulders, her own past raw in her throat. "Don't you dare blame either one of you. No one has the right to force themselves on another person. It's not anyone else's fault. Except Edgar's."

He put out a hand and brushed his fingers against her cheek.

"No. Of course not. I'm sorry, I didn't mean it that way. But I can't help but feel—I'm better off as things are and, god knows, Kitty is. But I let her down."

"I'm extraordinarily fond of Kitty." Odd to think now how jealous she'd been of Kitty when they'd first met. Malcolm's first love, a beautiful, self-possessed woman, seemingly without any cracks in her armor. "But you can't blame yourself for what she kept from you."

"Is that what you'd say if you were Kitty?"

Her own past raced through her mind. Secrets. Lies. Mistakes. Impossible decisions she regretted but might make again. "I'm quite sure Kitty doesn't blame you."

"No, she's far too generous. She might never have forgiven me over political disagreements, but she'd never hold personal failings over me." He scraped a hand over his dark hair. It flopped back over his forehead in that way that made him look like a schoolboy. And held echoes of Leo. And for very different reasons, Colin. "But it doesn't change what Leo faces. And it's—
"

"It's worse than what Colin has to contend with."

Malcolm returned her gaze steadily. "Colin's fine. He has two fathers and a mother and multiple adults who love him. There's nothing in the story of his birth to hurt him."

There was the fact that she'd lied to Malcolm about how she'd become pregnant before they married. There was the fact that Raoul, who had been Mélanie's spymaster, was Colin's biological father and also Malcolm's. But Malcolm was right. They'd managed to present it to Colin so that he focused on all the people involved loving him. And so lies and deceptions and spy missions weren't part of the story. Some day he would have more questions. But for now, they were managing.

Malcolm drew a breath. "I think I always knew my own parentage wasn't what I'd been told it was. It was a relief, in many ways. Realizing Alistair hadn't played a role in my conception. For many reasons."

"I can understand that. But you're yourself. And so is Leo."

"Easier though to think that than to understand it. Especially at Leo's age."

"Which is why Leo doesn't know the truth. He'll have to someday. But not until he's old enough to handle it."

Malcolm's mouth twisted. "I'm not sure one's ever old enough to handle it. But the secret being out makes the risks of his learning it greater." He hesitated. "I was always afraid Alistair would tell Leo. I still am."

Memories of those days when they'd confronted Alistair Rannoch swirled in her brain like fragments of glass. They'd scarcely been aware of what his goals were, yet beyond political power, beyond his trying to reclaim his fortune and Malcolm's inheritance—which Malcolm would have gladly given up—the fear that he'd try to claim Leo as his grandson had hung over all of them. "I think we all were."

Malcolm nodded. "But I didn't see the threat coming from this direction."

"Southcott prides himself on being a creature of the future. He's quite eager to look askance at his father and uncle and anyone of the past generation, whatever their political views. Yet though he may disdain the past, he's not afraid to make use of its secrets."

"No."

Mélanie's fingers tightened on her husband's arm. She looked into his familiar gray gaze and knew, as so often happened, that they were both thinking the same thing. But neither of them was ready to say it. For all it had been a truism of their lives. From that moment on a dusty stage when he confronted her about her past and the reasons she'd married him. The moment she had thought signaled the downfall of their marriage. The fact that it hadn't didn't change the truism.

Plan for the future all one wanted, one could never really escape the past.

~

Kitty looked down in the glow of the tin-shaded nursery night-light and touched her fingers to her elder son's hair. A honey gold now, rather than the platinum of his baby hair. When had it darkened? When had it got so thick? One didn't notice the day-by-day changes in the midst of coping with everyday life. She could see the shape of the man he'd become in the bones of his face, and also see echoes of the baby he'd been. Young enough to be vulnerable (was one ever not?). And old enough to understand so much. He wasn't the man who was his father in pure biology. She'd known that from the first and it was so clear watching him grow. Watching him influenced by other adults. Including Julien, whom he now called father. But he'd have questions about the past as he grew. Who wouldn't?

She pressed a kiss to his forehead, kissed Timothy and Genny, asleep in their beds, and patted Luna, their new puppy, asleep by Timothy's feet.

Julien, who usually moved beside her when she checked on the children, was waiting for her by the door to their bedchamber. He stepped aside as she moved into the room, then softly closed the door behind her.

Kitty turned to look at her husband. The light from the brace of candles he'd lit fell across the blue and gold of the carpet between them. "How much do you think Southcott knows?"

Julien put his hand on the closed door of the nursery. "I've been asking myself that over and over. On the one hand, he didn't give away details. Which might mean he doesn't have them and was simply striking out blind hoping he'd hit something. Or it might have been a clever way of protecting his intelligence and sources."

"Precisely. And someone took that page from Diego's letter to Caulfield-West. I think we have to assume it was Southcott. And I think we have to assume the worst about what it reveals. So—"

"So I think we have to assume—"

"That he knows everything." Saying it didn't change anything, but it tightened the fear in her chest.

"Kitkat—" Julien moved to her side and put a hand on her arm.

"It's all right, Julien." Kitty pulled away, then turned back to face him, arms folded over her chest. "That is, its's not all right at all, of course. It's my worst nightmare. But we've always known this could happen. I've known it longer than you. From the moment I realized I was pregnant. If we're not ready to handle it, now is the time to figure out a strategy."

"Getting the papers back seems a good strategy."

Kitty's fingers bit into her sleeves. She stared down at her white knuckles on the bronze-green satin. "Leo's going to have to know the truth at some point."

Julien stared at her as though she'd suggested handing over codes to the enemy. "Are you suggesting we tell him?"

The emerald ring Julien had given her when they married glinted in the candlelight. A memory of his mother. "It's the best response to blackmail and stolen intelligence, isn't it? To render the secret not a secret at all."

His gaze widened as though she'd suggested handing a code key with the codes. "You're talking about our—your—son."

Kitty looked into her husband's eyes. The bright blue had darkened to cobalt. "Our son. And you know facing hard truths about one's heritage better than anyone."

"I also know the value of a childhood. Perhaps because I never had one."

Kitty's breath caught. She put out a hand. "I didn't say—"

Julien strode to the hearthrug in front of the Carrara marble mantel his parents had commissioned in Italy on their wedding journey. Or his father had commissioned with his mother's dowry. He stared into the cold grate, then turned to face her. "Leo needs some more years of nurturing before he has to face the world. He'll be stronger for it."

Kitty held her husband's gaze. The ironic veil had lifted and echoes of untold childhood hurts shone through, raw and uncompromising. She could only guess at what showed in her own gaze. Her past was a prickly tangle. She'd already more than half left childhood behind at Leo's age, and by the time she was fifteen she'd had no illusions left. She hadn't shared the whole with anyone, though Julien knew more than most. "That's remarkable, Julien. And I quite agree. But while we can nurture him, I'm not sure we can protect him. I used to think I had to protect his relationship with Edward because lacking as Edward was as a father, he was the only father the boys had and it meant something to them. It's different now. They have you. You know the truth, and their knowing it can't hurt their relationship with you."

"No. But it's a lot for Leo to accept." Julien hesitated a moment, but he rarely shied from anything. "Knowing that the very fact of your existence hurt your mother."

"I'd never—"

"Of course not. But he has a keen understanding. There's no way to tell him the story without his realizing as much." Julien swallowed. "I dealt with the same, in a somewhat different way, about my own mother. She never should have married my father. I never should have been born. And I can only guess at how unpleasant the process of making me was."

"Julien." Kitty crossed to his side in two quick steps. "Your mother loved you." She touched his face. "You can't doubt that."

"Of course not. It doesn't change the fact that her life would have been much better if I hadn't been born. And I do understand that once I was born, she wouldn't have wanted to go back. At least, most of the time I can believe that. But one would like to spare Leo those battles at this point in his life."

Leo's sleeping face danced before Kitty's gaze. "I would as well. But if we can't control the narrative, we have to work on writing our own story."

"Granted. But let's not give up on controlling the narrative just yet."

"It's not easy to control a narrative. Especially when John Southcott is so determined to shape the story himself."

"No." Julien's hands moved to her shoulders. "But if anyone can manage it, we should be able to."

CHAPTER 8

Buenos Aires, The Argentine
February 1816

Kitty tossed down a sip of red wine. Fruity and rough with a raw edge. Very different from the bottles her husband had imported from France all through the war, managing his way round the blockade as so many English gentlemen did. It was one thing to swear to bring down Napoleon. Another to give up good wine. "I'm sorry. I'm not the easiest person to be round."

"I wouldn't say that." Julien relaxed back in his chair, his own glass tilting between his fingers. As though he might toss the contents on the ground, though she knew he wouldn't spill a drop. "And no one should have to worry about being easy to be round."

She shot a sideways glance at him. It was a long time since she'd been used to speaking easily to anyone. Except for those bursts of confidences she'd made to Luisa, around the time of Leo's birth. Mostly late at night and fueled by too many glasses of wine. Confidences that now seemed unwise. "We all have ghosts in our past. It helps sometimes to be with someone who doesn't know them."

"By all means." He took a drink of wine. "I have more ghosts than I can count. I ignore them most of the time. But they do have a damnable way of crowding in round the edges. I've got in the habit of living with them. Most of the time we can make peace."

She held his gaze. If she had secrets, so, evidently, did he. And he'd revealed even less to her than she had to him. His eyes were the blue of an Italian lake, but their expression shifted like a fathoms-deep ocean. And it was as difficult to read what lay in their depths. "And when you can't?"

"Ah, that's a challenge." He twisted the stem of his glass between his fingers, watching the bright sun shoot through the red of the wine. "There are a few nights I've tried to wrestle them into submission. It very seldom works."

"It's hard to imagine you failing at anything."

"Oh, I've failed at more things than I can count. The trick mostly is not letting it matter."

She curled her fingers round her own glass. "You've helped. Helped keep my ghosts in the past. Where they belong. Helped me live in the present."

"I'm glad. I don't need to know your past. But you deserve the best present possible."

"Doesn't everyone?"

He flung back his head and gave a rare, full-throated laugh. "I'm not sure I'd go that far."

She sought refuge in a quick drink of wine and stared into the depths of her glass. She'd never been the sort to waste energy on vengeance or recriminations. It interfered with getting on with living. And most people had things in their past to regret. But it was difficult to think about Edgar Rannoch with magnanimity. It was difficult to think about Edgar Rannoch at all.

"I thought it would be an escape," she said. "Going across the ocean. And it is, in a way. One can leave people and places behind. But one can't leave behind the memories."

"No," he agreed. "Whatever name one uses, however many disguises one dons. Those are the ghosts that won't be left behind."

He didn't know the truth. But he must guess some of it. The first night they'd made love—or tried to—she hadn't been able to continue. And he'd been remarkably matter of fact. He hadn't pushed her for answers, but they'd sat and talked and he'd seemed instinctively to know what would push past her barriers. But there were some secrets she'd never be able to confide. And god help her if they ever saw the light of day.

CHAPTER 9

London
July 1821

"Mr. Hubert Mallinson." Valentin said, as he opened the door of the breakfast parlor. Valentin had served in the Rannoch household for over six years, including through the Battle of Waterloo and the White Terror. He had shown tact and discretion in numerous investigations. But learning to call the former Lord Carfax "Mr. Hubert Mallinson" had shaken his equilibrium. He no longer hesitated over the name as he had in the first weeks. Malcolm admitted it still sounded a bit like someone's younger brother. Which Hubert was, taking Julien's father into account. But they'd all got used to the fact that whatever Hubert was called, he'd always be a force to be reckoned with.

"Hubert." Mélanie got up from the breakfast table. "We were wondering if we'd see you this morning."

Hubert paused on the threshold, gaze sweeping over the group gathered round the eggshells and toast crumbs and marmalade smears left on the table. His gaze settled on Julien and Kitty. "If you've been here all night, this is even more serious than I feared."

"We came this morning with the children," Kitty said. Neglecting to add that they'd only been home for a few hours before their return to Berkeley Square.

"In fact, Kitty and Laura and I were just about to check on the children in the library," Mélanie said. "If you'll excuse us. Malcolm, do give Hubert some coffee and ring for food if we need more."

Hubert watched the three women leave the breakfast parlor. "They'd only leave to check on the children if they wished to avoid the conversation."

"Quite." Malcolm poured a cup of coffee and handed it to his former spymaster. It was not yet ten, but it already felt like a long day.

Hubert accepted the coffee and took a grateful sip. "Where's O'Roarke?"

"He's already gone out." Malcolm set the coffeepot down and returned to his chair.

"Already on the case, is he?"

"What case?" Julien asked in a deceptively mild voice.

Hubert moved to a chair. "I assume you've heard from Southcott?" He clunked down his cup and saucer.

Normally, Malcolm would not lightly answer such a question from the man he had served for perhaps the most misspent years of his life. The man who had sent them into exile and was still a threat to Mélanie and Raoul. Not to mention Archie Davenport. But when it came to Southcott, Hubert was an ally. Which was not a word Malcolm had ever thought to associate with his former spymaster. "He called on us last night," Malcolm said. "Made sure we were all gathered together."

"All of you?" Hubert's gaze shot round the room as though seeking traces of the others who had been present the night before.

"Cordy and Harry, Tony and Désirée, Julien and Kitty, Harriet and Gresham. Jeremy and Judith. And all of us in Berkeley Square."

Hubert grunted. "I won't ask what he threatened to reveal, as you'd be fools to tell me. But I assume he threatened all of you."

"Decidedly." Julien folded his arms, leant back in his chair, and regarded his uncle. "I take it he also called on you with threats?"

Hubert picked up his coffee and tossed down another swallow. "Can you doubt it?"

"It had occurred to us," Malcolm said. "We were more than half expecting you to walk in last night along with everyone else. I suppose the reason he didn't include you with us is that if he'd revealed his threats to you in front of us, they wouldn't be threats so much anymore. And the same with talking to you without us."

"Quite." Hubert tugged at his spectacles. "It's a damned mess."

"You're the one who wanted to watch Southcott and see what his next move would be," Julien said. "Not that we can't still try to do so. We just have to make sure we don't get caught doing it. He's a bit lacking in finesse, but he's made it quite clear he won't hesitate to use his knowledge against us."

"That's the problem." Hubert pushed his spectacles up on his nose. "I'm beginning to think it would have been decidedly easier simply to eliminate him."

"I said you'd say that." Julien picked up the coffeepot and splashed more coffee into his uncle's cup. "Kitty pointed out he's probably planned for such an eventuality."

"Probably." Hubert stared into the depths of his cup. "It would help if he were stupider."

"You always complained we thought too much," Malcolm pointed out.

"It was the things you thought about. But I never denied your intelligence was helpful. Anyway, you weren't antagonists."

"Depends on when you're talking about." Julien refilled Malcolm's cup and then his own.

Hubert shot a look at him. "Just what are you admitting to?"

"I wasn't admitting to anything. You've been our antagonist more times than I can count. Mostly over threats to reveal secrets." Julien set the coffeepot down, hard enough to spatter coffee on the tablecloth. "You sent us running across the Channel. Well, Mélanie and Malcolm and O'Roarke and Laura running. Because of secrets I revealed to you."

"You revealed them to Sylvie St. Ives," Malcolm pointed out.

"Same thing, or I should have known it was the same thing." Julien pressed a napkin over the spilt coffee. "One of the worst of my many regrets."

"That's ancient history." Hubert tossed down a swallow of coffee.

"Define ancient," Julien said. "I don't think the Davenports would agree."

"And none of this settles what we're going to do about Southcott," Hubert added.

"Who said anything about 'we'?" Julien asked.

"In this, we're allies."

"We have goals in common." Malcolm set down his own coffee cup. "It's not necessarily the same thing."

"Don't play with words, Malcolm. We haven't the time for it. Common ground makes us allies, at least in this. What are you planning to do to counter Southcott? Steal the papers?"

"Who says there are papers?" Julien asked.

"There are always papers. And I have to say you're probably better at recovering them than anyone." Hubert's brows drew together.

"Wondering about our finding the papers about you?" Julien asked.

"I'd be a fool not to be. But all things considered, I'm more concerned with Southcott's having them."

"The papers about you?"

"The papers about anyone. It won't improve the situation if you go running off to Italy again. To own the truth, I was concerned Malcolm would have already."

"Don't think I didn't think about it," Malcolm said. "But I have a distinct dislike of giving way to a bully."

"Southcott has new ideas about how to run things." Hubert tugged at his spectacles' earpiece. "He drives me mad, but he may be the way of the future."

"Uncle Hubert." Julien pushed himself to his feet. "You aren't thinking of giving way to Southcott, of all people?"

Hubert regarded his nephew. "I should think the idea of my giving way to anyone would delight you no end."

"Not anyone. I'm not so undiscerning."

"But isn't your whole belief that I'm mired in the past? And Southcott is the future."

"I believe the term I used about you was 'trying to turn the clock back.' Which is a losing battle and a stupid one. But that doesn't mean anyone with a new vision is better. In fact, some new visions are decidedly worse. Southcott is not the future I want for my children or any of our friends' children. For any children at all."

Hubert's gaze shot over Julien's own. Challenging. Assessing. "Are you asking me to stay in the game?"

"I don't want you to leave the field because of Southcott. We need you to defeat him."

If it meant something to Hubert that his nephew had acknowledged needing him, he didn't express it. "And for the rest?"

"And for the rest, it will be up to us to defeat you on our own. I have great faith in my allies, if not in myself."

"Well, then." Hubert pushed his spectacles up on his nose. "What do you need me to do?"

"Seven words I never thought to hear come out of your mouth," Malcolm said.

"Nor I," Julien agreed.

"But it would be helpful if you stayed out of the way at the *Liliana* opening," Malcolm said.

"What the hell is the *Liliana* opening—oh, Gresham's opera." Hubert's brows drew together. "What does that have to do with Southcott?"

"He'll be there," Malcolm said. "Along with a good portion of the beau monde. Including the king."

"What does the king have to do with this?" A note of concern crept into Hubert's voice.

"Nothing," Malcolm said. A bit more firmly than he believed. "We hope. We need Southcott distracted during the opening."

"Oh." Hubert took a meditative sip of coffee. "Interesting time for a break-in, but I suppose you've thought it through. Not the most interesting assignment, but I'll do my best."

"You haven't been a field agent for years," Julien said.

"That you know of." Hubert set down his cup.

"Fair enough, uncle. Far be it from me to deny your talents. And we can use them to distract Southcott. We'll handle the rest. The less you know, the better."

"Meaning you don't want me anywhere near the papers."

Julien lifted his coffee cup to his uncle. "But of course."

CHAPTER 10

"*R*annoch." Tristram Gresham got up from a table in the King's Theatre, Haymarket, where he was making notes on a score, and walked to the edge of the stage as Malcolm approached.

"Sorry to interrupt," Malcolm said. "I know what it's like the day before opening. Mélanie would snap my head off for interrupting."

"I'm sure she wouldn't, and I'm sure you wouldn't be so ill-judged as to interrupt. At least, not without urgent cause. It's all right, we're on a break." Gresham swung down off the stage. "What is it? More details about tomorrow?"

"We're wondering about the timing of the first act."

"Oh, that's easy. I can give you a notated score, with the best time for the mission to start clearly marked."

Malcolm met Tristram's gaze, as he would with a fellow agent plotting a mission. Which was more or less the case. "It's an important night. With the king there."

"I don't give a damn about the king," Gresham said, without the least care of who heard him among the singers, orchestra members, and stagehands scattered round the theatre. "Look, I know patrons are important. I'm fortunate to have an independent income, but I can't fund a whole opera. But honestly, any distraction at the opening will just make the opera more talked about."

"You're remarkably calm." Malcolm was well accustomed now to his wife's nerves before one of her plays premiered.

"About the opening? Oh, I'm in a fairly constant state of panic. But I've been through it. Even as I toss and turn through the night, a part of me knows that it will subside, the opera will open, and I'll stop regretting the dozens of things I'm now questioning. It's a familiar panic. Quite unlike—"

Malcolm watched Gresham in the hazy light of the rehearsal lamps. "Yes?"

"It's different when it's a risk one's never taken before. With someone else's happiness at stake." Gresham hesitated, fingers moving over a seat back. "How did you know?"

"Know what?" Malcolm said.

"That you were ready to make the leap." Gresham hesitated again, as though trying to find the right key for a new aria. "Committing to one person."

Malcolm felt himself smile. "I wouldn't say it was really a leap. We married in the middle of a war. In—pressing circumstances."

"But you didn't take the commitment lightly." Gresham's gaze was unusually steady. "I can tell that. It's plain about you."

"No. Though I was afraid I'd be a miserable failure as a husband."

"I can't imagine your being unfaithful."

"Not in the obvious way. I didn't—" Malcolm bit back the words. He liked Gresham, but he wasn't ready to admit he'd only had one lover prior to Mélanie, let alone that that lover was Kitty, now happily married to Julien. Kitty, whose secrets they were trying to protect. Secrets that existed due to the crimes of Malcolm's brother. "I didn't think I'd be physically unfaithful. I didn't think I'd be very good at sharing myself. I'm not very good at sharing myself even now."

Gresham's gaze narrowed. With surprising understanding, given the varied nature of their romantic pasts. "I've never quite put it that way. But I'm not either. One doesn't need to share oneself with—er—transient relationships. And when there's any sort of espionage involved, one can't." He cast a look at Malcolm as though to ask if Malcolm had experienced that, then seemed to understand. Odd to feel so vulnerable and at the same time so grateful for the understanding. "I never felt I had to hide with Harriet. Well, I never could hide. She saw through me the moment she walked into the sitting room in Désirée's cottage."

"The way I've heard her tell it, you saw through her as well."

"Perhaps. We both know what it is to have a facade. And we've both found it useful in our work." Gresham cast a glance towards the orchestra pit, where the musicians were going over bits of the score during the break. "Perhaps that's why I knew I couldn't have anything transient with Harriet. Oh, I was worried about what it would do to her. I'm not entirely without scruples. But I also knew there'd be no hiding anything between us. In any way. Which would make it completely different from anything I'd known with a lover before. Remarkable and terrifying. But I wasn't sure I could be what I needed to be to make it work."

A violinist had started to pick out a melody in a minor key. A fragment from the opera that made one's heart jump in one's throat. "I wasn't either," Malcolm said. "In fact, I was sure I wasn't. I'd never have taken the risk of marrying Mel—or anyone—if it weren't for exigent circumstances."

Gresham met his gaze for a moment, his own gaze remarkably open, and nodded. "For all the terror, when I realized what I wanted it was a tremendous relief. I keep hearing that it's a terrible risk, that I can't be sure I'll be a good—even a decent— husband. And it's not that I don't worry. I just told you I doubt myself. But on the inside I feel the most ridiculous optimism." He scraped a hand over his hair. "Not the first time I've been accused of insanity."

"Some of the greatest insights come from those deemed insane. Only think of Don Quixote. Or Hamlet."

Gresham laughed. "I can hardly claim such ideals. Merely an absurd belief in a happiness I never really considered possible."

"Hamlet might have done a lot better if he could have believed in happiness."

"A good point. I have a feeling my next opera will be a comedy." Gresham stared across the theatre for a moment. "She deserves to be happy. She deserves better than me. But improbably I'm what she seems to want."

"That is quite apparent. And shows her remarkable good sense."

"You're a good fellow, Rannoch. But that's going too far."

"On the contrary. I'd call it remarkably discerning to recognize a kindred spirit."

Gresham held his gaze for a moment and flushed. "Talking of discerning. You're quite discerning yourself."

"When the wind is southerly."

CHAPTER 11

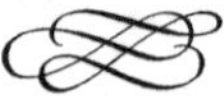

Southampton Road
Two Weeks Earlier

Tristram swung up into the carriage. The frame creaked and the interior lamps swayed. "The Delaneys definitely went through here. Bound for London."

Harriet tightened her grip on her reticule. Information at least gave them a goal. Even if they'd been going in the wrong direction. "So we turn round. At least we know we're headed in the right direction now."

Tristram gave a quick, contained nod.

"I'm sorry." She put out a hand as he dropped onto the seat opposite her. "I've led you on a wild goose chase. And you've missed rehearsal."

"It's not that." Tristram rapped on the roof of the carriage to signal the coachman to start. "We left in the middle of the night. We might have got away with that, no one would have known quite when we left. But now we definitely won't be back until another night has passed."

"Yes, as I said, I'm very sorry you've missed a rehearsal—"

"Damn it, not that—"

"Then what—Oh." Harriet sat back against the squabs. The carriage was well sprung and upholstered in soft watered silk. He'd probably brought all sorts of women in here. For all sorts of reasons. "That."

"Yes, damn it, that."

"Well, it's silly. This emphasis on overnight. I mean, we could have done anything we like the moment we left without waiting for darkness—" She broke off and felt warmth suffuse her cheeks.

"For that matter, we could have done it in my rooms before we left," Tristram said.

She forced herself to meet his gaze. "Yes, quite."

"But as with so many things, it isn't the reality but the appearance that counts."

"It's absurd—"

"And as with so many things, rail as we may, we have to deal with the world we live in."

"The rules are absurd, the world is absurd, and I don't care in the least."

He held her gaze across the carriage, his own glittering in the light of the interior lamps. "*I* care."

She returned his gaze for as long as she dared, aware they were treading round something challenging. Something they were going to have to confront at some point. Challenging as it was to teeter, as they had been, on a wobbly line between friends and lovers, it also had given them a safe space to linger in, a space she suspected he was even more reluctant to leave than she was. "Why start caring now?"

Tristram gripped the carriage strap as they rounded a corner. "I'm a libertine, not a cad—I hope. I'd have worried about being away overnight with anyone. Gossip can be faced down, but there are certain blatant lines one can't get away with crossing."

"You sound as though you've given this a great deal of thought."

"My dear." His eyes glinted in the shadows. "With the life I lead, I've had to."

"You're a man and an aristocrat, Tristram. When it comes to love affairs, there aren't really any rules you have to follow."

"I may be incapable of fidelity, but I'm not heartless. Not quite."

"Of course not. You're a bit of a fraud. That was clear to me from the first."

"My sweet." A light flashed in his eyes as the carriage swayed. "You saw through me from the first, in many ways. But I am undoubtedly a libertine."

"Well, yes. You're just a lot of other things. And not nearly so heedless as you let on." Harriet folded her arms beneath her cloak. "I'm glad you're not just careful round me. I wouldn't want to be treated differently."

"No?" His gaze glinted again, in a way that did uncomfortable things to her insides.

"Well, not in this way. It wouldn't reflect very well on you if you were only considerate of me."

The squabs creaked as he leant his head back. "You're a remarkable woman, Harriet. I'll do my best to keep this from becoming a scandal."

"Yes, that would be tiresome. But really, we couldn't have let fear of scandal stand in the way of helping friends."

Tristram turned his head and met her gaze, something oddly soft in his own. "No, we couldn't have done."

"So we're agreed. We really aren't so different after all."

"My darling," Tristram said, and then drew in his breath as though at an admission. "You have no idea."

CHAPTER 12

London
July 1821

"Tristram." Harriet tightened her fingers on the blue superfine on her betrothed's sleeve as they made their way down Pall Mall after the rehearsal.

"Mmm?" From the look in Tristram's eyes, he was still puzzling over the third act trio.

"Do you remember what we said the night we drove back after looking for the Delaneys?"

He cast a quick sideways glance at her, gaze glinting. "We said a number of things that night."

"About the fact that we were gone overnight."

"Yes, we seem to have avoided any talk that was too dramatic. Of course, our engagement provided a new source of gossip."

"You said that was one of those lines one couldn't cross."

"Sadly and idiotically true."

"You were panicked."

"No. Yes. The thing is, I knew we were playing with something that could destroy both of us. We'd been playing with it for weeks."

"You thought we couldn't be together if we weren't married."

"Not exactly."

"Well, you certainly avoided letting anything go further." She remembered those days. Smiles. Leaning against his shoulder while they worked. His arm settling round her. An occasional quick kiss. Sometimes a bit more than quick. But always pulling back before it could go too far. Sometimes sitting on the frayed sofa in that basement sitting room at the Tavistock Theatre curled in his arms. Teetering on the edge of something neither of them dared voice. Aware a decision lay ahead of them, but both of them putting it off because they weren't ready to face what that might mean.

"Damn it, we were in the basement of the Tavistock. We didn't even have a bed."

"Tristram, you can't tell me you couldn't have found a bed if you'd put your mind to it."

"That isn't how I wanted it to be."

Harriet tilted her head to the side to look up at him round the brim of her bonnet. "I was afraid I was going to have to seduce you."

"Afraid?"

"No, not really, actually. I'd made up my mind to it." She'd thought of it on that drive back on the Southampton Road after their wild goose chase after the Delaneys. Curled up against Tristram with her head on his shoulder. Realizing they had to break this frozen stalemate and she was going to have to be the one to do it. "I was rather—excited, actually."

"Well, that's a relief." He gave a faint smile.

"I was fairly sure I could get past your qualms of conscience. But was the reason we were away overnight why you—"

"Why I what?" Tristram was scanning the street ahead, crowded with late afternoon traffic. He must have been aware of her regard, because he stopped in front of a swinging sign for a bookseller's and turned his head again to stare at her. "You can't think—"

Harriet looked steadily into his gaze. The light was behind him, making his expression hard to read beneath the curling brim of his hat. "You're very careful of reputations. You've been particularly careful of my reputation. But if you thought that meant you had to—"

"Harriet." Tristram laid his hand over her own where it rested on his sleeve. "I bought the diamond pendant long before you came to me wanting to go after the Delaneys. It was meant as an engagement present. I was just trying to find the right way to ask you. And wondering if you'd say yes."

She felt a smile break across her face as relief coursed through her. Still—"You'd say that anyway."

"Possibly. But you can't deny I'd already bought the pendant. I'd have asked you that night, but I couldn't very well in the midst of everything." His fingers tightened over her own. "You may question your sanity in marrying me. But I have no doubts about wanting to marry *you*."

Sometimes, when he looked at her like that, she couldn't contain her breathing. "You always know just what to say." She kept her voice light in an effort at self-command.

"On the contrary. I've bungled more times than I can count."

"That's only because—"

Harriet broke off, suddenly aware of the pressure of multiple gazes. Two ladies with shopping parcels were staring at them from across the street. Another lady in a high-crowned sapphire bonnet and matching spencer trimmed with black braid was regarding them from the steps of a mantua maker's two doors down.

Tristram had caught the lady's eye. Harriet felt a faint tremor run through his arm. He paused and lifted his hat. "Mrs. Atwood."

"Lord Gresham." The lady descended the remainder of the steps. She was tall and slender and the hair that showed beneath her the silk-lined brim of her bonnet was a smooth, pale blonde.

"I don't believe you know Miss Roth?" Tristram said. "Mrs. Atwood. An old friend."

Mrs. Atwood smiled—a cool, practiced smile—and inclined her head to Harriet. "Miss Roth. A pleasure. I confess I've been very curious to meet you. My felicitations to you both on your engagement. You are quite the talk of London."

"You're too kind," Harriet said in a bright voice she'd perfected since her betrothal to Tristram had become pubic. "But then Tristram has always been the center of attention. And I don't believe I ever will be."

"You underrate yourself, Miss Roth. The woman who captured Tristram Gresham could hardly fail to become the center of attention."

"I protest." Tristram flung out his free arm in one of his extravagant gestures. "While I might be quite capable of allowing myself to be captured, Harriet doesn't believe in capturing anyone."

Mrs. Atwood gave a thin smile. "Very clever, Tristram. You haven't changed a bit. I doubt you ever will. My compliments to you both."

She turned and swept up to a sapphire barouche where a footman was waiting to hand her up the steps.

Tristram released a rough breath. "I'm sorry."

"It's hardly the first time. And it won't be the last, I'm sure." Harriet had grown quite inured to encountering Tristram's former mistresses. "What else does one expect when one becomes betrothed to a rake?" She frowned as she watched Mrs. Atwood's barouche pull away down the street. "I think I've just realized who she is. Malcolm and Mélanie know her. And she's connected to the Mallinsons."

"Honoria Talbot Atwood. Hubert Mallinson is her uncle."

"That's right. Julien calls her 'my poisonous cousin Honoria.'"

Tristram arced a brow. "Julien has an adept way of putting things."

"She's very lovely. Rather the same type as Rosalind Azevado, actually. Your taste does seem to run to blondes."

"My taste doesn't run to any type in particular. Except sharp-tongued, distractingly lovely brunettes at present."

Tristram was the one who was distracting, but Harriet wasn't going to let herself be distracted. "Her husband's a diplomat, isn't he? Was that the reason for the affair?"

"Keen as ever, my sweet. They'd been in Italy. They were close to Metternich—Honoria rather closer than her husband, from what I'd heard, and that seems to have been true. She likes challenges. I don't think she found me much of a challenge."

"It isn't like you to sell yourself short."

"Statement of fact. Honoria's taste runs to men who are difficult to seduce. Which I hardly was. Especially since I'd set my sights on seducing her. Unfortunately, I think now she's decided I'm a challenge after all."

"Why would she—Oh."

"I never thought that being a devoted spouse-to-be would make one attractive. I suppose I should have, though."

"How convenient."

"It's not convenient in the least. It's damned tiresome. I begin to be distinctly sympathetic to Rannoch."

"Why—" Harriet's eyes widened. "Oh. Did she actually—"

"Oh yes. I don't know all the details, but she and Malcolm grew up together. She set her sights on him years ago. And she failed, which of course made him all the more intriguing. And made her convinced he was the love of her life." Tristram regarded her for a moment. "That isn't why I—"

"Well, no, of course not. It's not as though I resisted."

"Mmm. You weren't in the least interested in me at the start."

"I wouldn't say that precisely. But I had more important

things to think about than a love affair that was going to create all sorts of complications."

"Precisely."

"But later I was quite ready to have an affair. You were the one with scruples. Which I have to say rather frustrated me more than intrigued me."

"Plainspoken as always."

"It's a compliment, dearest."

"Of a sort."

"It must have been beastly for Malcolm. He's not the sort who would ever give way to seduction. His scruples would make yours look paltry."

"Thank you. And you're quite right."

"And it must be beastly for Mélanie."

"It was before they met, I believe."

"No, not that. I imagine Honoria Talbot Atwood is just her image of the sort of girl Malcolm would have married if he'd had a conventional life."

"I'm sure Mélanie's too sensible to imagine Malcolm would have been remotely happy with a conventional life."

"It's not like that, darling." Harriet turned, heedless of the passersby, and put her hands on his chest. "One cannot but imagine alternate stories. Mélanie started as an outsider in this world. And their"—she hesitated because, much as she trusted Tristram, close as they were, there were secrets she wasn't sure it was her right to share. Especially because they weren't things she knew, but things she had pieced together from bits of knowledge. She believed in theorizing, but a theory wasn't fact. "Their marriage didn't have a conventional start. Even now one hears talk. I'm sure she wonders sometimes at the life he'd have had if he hadn't met her."

"Whereas I imagine Rannoch is thanking his lucky stars—or would be, if he believed in anything so absurd—that he met her and she saved him from a sadly conventional fate."

"Very likely, but it won't change things for her. Honoria Talbot Atwood is the sort of woman who would haunt her."

Tristram's gaze flickered over face. "Are you saying that you—"

"No, dearest. I can't really imagine you with a conventional woman. It's enough of a stretch of the imagination to imagine you with me."

He laughed. "I'm afraid Honoria is going to be tiresome. I hadn't quite thought that however much we may laugh at my past, it's going to intrude on our present."

"Only if we let it."

"I fear we can't ignore the world, my sweet. We can laugh at it, but it's still there. We have to build our lives round it."

"*Our* lives. We needn't listen to others."

"No, but unless we hide in the country, they'll be hard to ignore. And we're neither of us the sort to hide. Though one does start to sympathize with Tony and Désirée."

"They'll find it hard to hide too."

"So they will." Harriet turned and curled her gloved fingers round Tristram's arm as they started walking again across St. James's Square. "Fortunately or unfortunately, they're both used to living on a public stage."

"And I'm not."

"You live in the midst of the world while staying in the shadows. There's a lot to be gained from avoiding notice."

"That's why you've tried so hard to do it?"

"I've never held myself up as a shining example of—anything."

"But I also think you weren't unhappy in the full blaze of attention. In fact, you'd be quite lost without it."

"I'm not—"

"Mmm. You like playing to an audience, my love. I knew that when I took you on."

"I don't mind having my past thrown in my face. I just don't want it thrown in yours."

"I don't think there's any avoiding it. I told you, the past doesn't bother me."

"None of them were—"

"Don't say none of them meant anything to you, Tristram. That won't make me think well of you."

"I was going to say none of them was you."

"Statement of fact."

"This is different. You do believe that, don't you?"

"My love. I wouldn't be marrying you otherwise."

"I was prepared for gossip. I wasn't prepared for people to be spiteful."

"Then you don't understand gossip. Or the beau monde. It's all right." Harriet smiled at him. "I'm used to being an outsider."

Tristram tightened his fingers on her arm. "I wish I could have spared you this."

"Don't talk nonsense, Tristram. You know I can't abide the thought of being protected."

"Really?" He drew back and looked down at her. "I quite like the idea you'd try to protect me. But I suppose I'm not nearly as stalwart as you are."

"You have the most wonderful way of talking nonsense."

"Thank you. I do try. But I'd have given a great deal to have protected you from this."

"You're very clever, Tristram. But I'm not sure that even you are capable of such a Herculean feat. Gossip is inevitable."

"I'm used to gossip. I hoped it would stay focused on me."

"But as a dramatist you should recognize that I'm part of the story. And much less known than you, so there are more things to speculate about. Not to mention people being jealous. I mean, I imagine a lot of women have hoped to marry you."

"Ha. More sensible to run a mile from me. And I categorically deny I ever gave anyone the sense I had the least interest in marriage. In fact, I went out of my way to make the opposite clear."

"Which only made you all the more intriguing. This game can be played more than one way, my love. If it's a challenge to seduce a woman who resists, it's equally a challenge to get a confirmed rake to commit to marriage."

"For someone who's never played this particular game, you have a lot of insights."

"I'm a good observer. And especially once we started going about in the beau monde, I could see a lot. As we've discussed, it's very helpful to be able to fade into the background."

"Mmm. Distinctly. But I never tried to seduce women who resisted. I had no interest in ruining reputations. Or marriages that weren't already ruined."

"Yes, my love. You're a far better person than you let on. It doesn't change the fact that dozens of women have probably imagined securing you."

"What a ghastly word. Mamas of marriageable daughters generally avoid me like the plague."

"And that makes you all the more intriguing to the daughters."

CHAPTER 13

Tony adjusted a fold in the cravat he had just tied with effortless elegance. Désirée had learnt to be quite passable at tying a cravat while masquerading as a man on missions, but she had to admit she didn't have Tony's panache.

As though aware of her regard, Tony met her gaze in the looking glass. "Do you trust him?"

"Tristram?" Désirée snapped closed the links on her citrine-and-diamond bracelet. "With what? With secrets? I have, more than once. With my safety and, more importantly, Sophie's. I did when we left France, and he didn't let us down. There are few people I'd have trusted in that situation. Few people you'd have trusted."

Tony turned from the mirror and looked at her directly. "With Harriet."

"I think that's a question for Harriet."

"You know what I mean. I have no doubt that he loves her. No doubt that he intends to change."

"But you don't believe he really can?" Désirée moved to stand beside him at the mirror so she could adjust her diamond filagree bandeau. The *Liliana* opening would mark the most major appearance she and Tony had made in London. And they had a part to play in tonight's mission. Costume was vital to a good performance.

"Do you?"

"I've changed." She coaxed a ringlet to fall so it didn't hide her citrine earrings. "At least, you seem to believe I have. Do you trust me?"

"Not to break my heart? Oh, yes. But with you, I think it was more strategic—"

"Oh, I think Tristram's love affairs have been plenty strategic." Désirée pulled another ringlet loose to fall over the bandeau. "Though I will admit he's been rather more—extravagant—than I ever was."

"Precisely. You didn't—"

"Flaunt my love affairs? No, that's true. I also didn't exaggerate them. Which I rather think Tristram did. That sort of exaggeration enhances a man's reputation and damages a woman's." She turned her head to see if she'd achieved the right degree of artfully disheveled coiffure. "But if you mean Tristram's catalogue is probably longer than mine, I have no doubt that it is."

"Will you roll your eyes if I say I'm relieved to hear it?"

"Darling." Désirée turned and put a hand on his silver waistcoat.

"I'm serious, sweetheart. I've become very fond of Harriet. I'm fond of Gresham as well. But —"

"You think a past as a rake makes someone incapable of fidelity?"

"You can't claim it wouldn't be an adjustment. That is—" The sort of questions they never put into words shot through his gaze.

"It's all right, Tony. Being with you is quite complicated enough to take my mind off anything else. But do you think men aren't as capable of fidelity as women?"

"No! Of course not."

She reached up and linked her hands behind his neck. "No one can know for a certainty what they may do in the future, Tony. But I'm quite determined to make our relationship"—

"Marriage—"

"—marriage—work. I truly believe Tristram is wholeheartedly committed to making his relationship with Harriet work. Of course, we can't know for a certainty where life will take any of us."

"But you choose to believe in him."

"Yes, I choose to."

"You're a closet romantic, Désirée."

"I never said I didn't believe in romance."

Tony quirked a brow at her.

"Just because I didn't indulge in maudlin fantasies—"

"Désirée."

"Well, it's one thing to believe in the possibility of love enduring under the right circumstances. Anyone remotely sane would have doubted it was likely to do so when it came to us."

"My point precisely. I mean, not that it was unlikely, but that you—"

"Tony. Can you blame me for trying to avoid having my heart broken?"

"You have to be a romantic to admit the possibility of a heart's being broken."

"Caught." Désirée touched the side of his face. "Loving's always a risk, Tony. But I'm willing to admit the risk is worth it now. And I think Harriet and Tristram would say the same. It amazes me every day that you're willing to take the risk of loving me."

"Oh, that's really not a risk at all. Life is impossibly dull without you."

"Another word for chaos."

"Honestly, I wasn't really living until I met you."

"Liar."

"Truly." He kissed her nose. "I was existing, but it was a hollow life."

"A very luxurious hollow life where you got to indulge your passion for spycraft."

"Oh, yes. I don't deny my good fortune. I don't regret a number of things—especially my children. But I found myself when I met you."

"People don't find themselves in another person, Tony."

"No. But you made me see possibilities for who I could be."

"Well, then." She put her hands on his chest. "I think Harriet may have done that for Tristram."

CHAPTER 14

"Uncle Simon! Uncle David!" Jessica jumped off Mélanie's lap and ran across the box to fling her arms round Simon Tanner and then David Mallinson. At four and a half, she was now tall enough to hug their waists. Mélanie could remember a not-too-distant past when her daughter would throw her arms round people's knees.

Two-year-old Clara O'Roarke jumped off her sister Emily's lap and ran to Simon, who scooped her up. Emily, seven, followed to hug the new arrivals, careful of her new sarcenet and tulle dress.

Simon, still holding Clara, bent to kiss Mélanie's cheek. "You look exquisite."

"I'm missing half my hair pins." She was wearing a new gown, pomegranate gauze over satin with a rose gold sash. With Blanca gone, she'd left her hair in loose ringlets at the back as she often did, and Jessica had pulled several pins from her coiffure.

"It will set a new style." Simon dropped onto a gilded chair beside her, Clara in his lap. "I wish you could set style for people actually listening to the opera. The couple behind us talked all through Liliana and Liam's duet."

"Oh, that's nothing." David moved to another chair. Jessica climbed into his lap and Emily sat beside him. "A lady with her opera glasses trained on the royal box blocked my view for half of the first act. At least Danielle Darnault still sounded glorious even if we couldn't always see her."

"I've wanted to see her as Liliana ever since I first heard a fragment of the score," Mélanie said. Which had been when she and Danielle called on Tristram in the course of an investigation. Danielle Darnault, like so many of their friends, was a former agent (though the 'former' was always questionable). She was also one of the most brilliant opera singers in Europe, and Tristram had written Liliana for her.

"She's brilliant. Also much more aesthetically pleasing than our sovereign." Simon glanced towards the king's box. "It looks as though Fanny's making sure the opera finds royal favor."

Frances Davenport, Malcolm's aunt, was seated beside the king, who appeared to be laughing at whatever she was saying. Fanny's husband Archie was still in their box, giving a sip of his champagne to Fanny's twelve-year-old daughter Chloe. They had all been doing their best to keep any hint of the night's mission—and John Southcott's threats—from Archie and Fanny. Both would find it impossible to stay out of it, which would only put Archie even more at risk. "Fanny always knows just what to do," Mélanie said.

"So she does." David smiled at Mélanie. "Everything all right?"

"Of course. Why shouldn't it be?"

"David's being diplomatic." Simon detached his cravat from Clara's fingers and gave her his watch chain to play with. "He's trying to say we both have the sense something's afoot."

"Father's here." David's gaze went to the box across the theatre where Hubert Mallinson sat with his wife Amelia,

David's mother, and David's youngest sister Lucinda. At least Lucinda had been there when the opera started. She must have gone to speak with friends during the interval because now Mélanie only saw Hubert and Amelia talking with Lord and Lady Londonderry.

"Hubert's always been suspicious of Tristram Gresham," Mélanie pointed out.

"You mean he thinks Radical plots are encoded in the score?" David demanded.

"He's thought stranger things about Radical plots," Simon said.

David glanced at the next box over. Colin, Mélanie's son, and Sophie, Désirée and Tony's daughter, had joined Kitty and Julien's children in their box. "Julien and Kitty left. And Raoul and Laura."

"They went to get ices for us." Emily smoothed the pink-embroidered moss green of her skirt. "With Malcolm. And champagne too, I think. But that not for us. The champagne, that is."

"Well said," Simon told her. "Lots of words are good for diversion."

"You're very observant," Mélanie said.

"We're amateurs," David said. "But we can't help but notice. We have picked up a bit being round you lot."

"Can we help?" Simon asked.

"You can help immeasurably by keeping up the illusion that there's nothing more to gossip about than Tristram and Harriet's betrothal."

"Plenty to gossip about there," Simon said. "Fortunate."

"Simon." David stared at his lover. "It must be hell for Tristram and Harriet."

"They're wise enough to know there's no escaping it. And generous enough to be more than willing to lend their scandal as cover, I imagine."

"We can't wish more talk on them," David said. "Good god!"

"What?" Simon asked.

"Harriet's just gone into John Southcott's box."

John looked up in quick surprise as she came into the box. Harriet let the curtains fall shut behind her. Good. She had an advantage.

"Miss Roth." He got to his feet and inclined his head. "I trust you are in good health."

"Yes, thank you." She moved to one of the gilded chairs and seated herself. At an angle that should obscure Julien and Kitty's box. If John stayed where he was. "I never thought you liked opera."

"Do people come to the opera because they like it?" John returned to his seat, flicking back the tails of his coat. "It's a place to be seen. Though I must say your betrothed's music is powerful."

"That's generous of you."

His gaze fastened on her face. For a moment, she could remember him handing her a cup of coffee in Covent Garden, the wind blowing the scent of flowers and garlic in their faces. "You're really going through with it?"

"We've always disagreed about a number of things, John. More than we acknowledged, it seems, based on recent events."

"Harriet—" He put out a hand, then let it fall to his biscuit-colored pantaloons. "We've always had different interests. Life has clearly taken us in different directions."

"You always put things so diplomatically, John."

"But I care about you." He drew in his breath and released it. "I always will. And however different we are, I can't believe you can be happy with a man like Gresham."

"John—" For a moment he was the friend she had sipped

coffee with. Then all the things she now knew he had done rushed into her mind. "I'm not sure you ever understood what would make me happy."

He coughed. "Are you saying you were looking for a man like—"

"I wasn't looking for any man," she said with perfect truth. "A month ago, I'd have told you marriage was the last thing I wanted. But Tristram and I understand each other."

"If you mean you'll give him license to—"

"Oh, no. I mean, we've always thought alike. I think that's what first intrigued him—that I can see through him. But he can see through me."

"He's going to break your heart, Harriet."

"Well, I suppose he might. There's no denying being in love makes one shockingly vulnerable. That's probably a large part of why I resisted it for so long. But he's risking just as much."

"Harriet, I don't think Gresham—"

"You don't think he could possibly be in love with me?" She smiled as she said it. In truth, she knew it was what a lot of people were thinking.

"You must know I—I could never question the feelings you might inspire in anyone. But a man like Gresham—Whatever feeling a woman may inspire in him. Whatever his intentions. He doesn't change his essential nature."

Harriet adjusted the heart-shaped diamond pendant Tristram had given her. "Oh, I quite agree with you there. I think Tristram's essential nature is very much as it has always been. What that means for our future is something I can't claim to know."

"You don't sound worried."

"Well, I'm not, actually. I know Tristram. And I choose to believe we can be happy together." She let her shawl trail over the back of the chair, where it would help hide the view behind her.

"Harriet. I realize how this must seem like a fairy tale—"

"John. Did you just accuse me, of all people, of believing in fairy tales?"

"Or something out of a novel—"

"If it was, it would be one of Laura O'Roarke's. I don't have the least illusion that Tristram is some figure of romance or that I've somehow saved him from himself. I wouldn't want to. I wouldn't want him to be other than himself."

Surprise flashed in John's eyes. "Then—"

"What we have took us by surprise. Both of us."

John's brows drew together. "I suppose I shouldn't be surprised that a man like Gresham would appeal to any woman—"

"Oh, John." She leant an elbow on the chair arm and tilted her head to the side, blocking a bit more of Julien and Kitty's box. "Do you think I fell in love with a rake?"

"Are you saying you didn't?"

"Well, I suppose technically—"

"I believe it's not uncommon for a woman to think she can reform a man who has resisted matrimony—"

"Oh, John." Harriet's shoulders hunched in genuine laughter. "If you think I've succumbed to the eternal lure of taming Don Giovanni—"

"Haven't you?"

"I wouldn't want Don Giovanni in the least. He has no interest in a woman's mind."

"If you're saying Gresham—"

"Well, I don't mean that's the only thing he's interested in. I don't mean that I'd want it to be. But I haven't the least expectation of changing Tristram. "

"He's a dangerous man."

"He believes in things. Far more than he lets on. So do I."

John looked steadily at her. "Harriet. We're in the midst of a very complicated game."

"A game in which you and I are on opposite sides."

"I can't argue with that. But take my advice, as a friend. Or if you won't call me a friend, as someone who wishes you well. Stay off the field. It's not safe for you."

"John." She held her own gaze as steady. "You must know I'll take that as a challenge."

"Don't, Harriet." His eyes had gone hard as agate. "You must know what I feel for you. But this is larger than that. This is a battle I can't afford to lose."

"Odd. Tristram said much the same to me once. But he meant it very differently."

"You've picked dangerous friends. But you don't have to play their games."

"They aren't games. I take this very seriously."

"So do I. But all politics is a game. One plans one's strategy accordingly. And a sensible person knows when it's better to sit on the sidelines. Cheering, perhaps. But not participating."

"I'm not a coward, John."

He leant towards her. "I can't protect you, Harriet."

"I don't want to be protected by anyone."

"Not even Gresham?"

"Perhaps especially not Tristram."

"I mean what I say, Harriet."

Harriet smiled and met his gaze like a sword cut. "So do I, John."

CHAPTER 15

$\mathcal{H}$enrietta, Duchess of Bamford, came through the curtains into the box where Désirée and Tony were sitting with Harry and Cordelia. She let the gold damask snap shut behind her with the force of a door being slammed to. Désirée silently applauded Hetty's technique. She might never have performed in a theatre, but she had a superb grasp of stagecraft. After all, the political and diplomatic world were one big stage.

"Hetty." Tony bowed to the woman who was still his wife. "A pleasant surprise."

"Don't you dare, Tony." Hetty took a step forwards, crystal-beaded gray silk whipping round her. "I didn't think you would sink so low." Her gaze snapped to Désirée.

"By going to the theatre?" Tony moved between Hetty and Désirée. "We all agreed to be civilized."

"And stay in our own spaces." Hetty's diamond earrings and necklace flashed in the candlelight as she shook with outrage. "It was one thing to be civilized when you stayed quietly in the country. It's quite another to come to the opening of the opera that I championed, with music that premiered in our house—with that woman in tow."

"That woman will soon be the Duchess of Bamford."

"Don't remind me."

"Tony." Désirée put a hand on her lover's—betrothed's—arm.

"I won't stand by and let her insult you." Tony looked at Hetty. "A scene will only make things worse."

"Oh, don't you try that. You were willing enough to make a scene parading your inamorata about. This is my territory," Hetty said. "I've lived my life in London society while you gallivanted all over the Continent and got up to god knows what. Soon I'll be a divorced woman and not invited half the places I once was. I'm resigned to it. I don't really have a choice, given what you're set on. But tonight was mine. My chance to reign over society one last time. And you couldn't even let me have that."

"We didn't think—" Désirée broke off, a genuine qualm shooting through her. Hetty had been keen to help them. But what tonight might mean to her hadn't occurred to Désirée until now.

"You didn't think at all, that's the problem," Hetty said.

"Perhaps some champagne." Cordelia moved forwards with a rustle of silk. "I know how challenging these times can be."

"I imagine you do, Lady Cordelia," Hetty said. "But at least you were sensible enough to live your life well away from Colonel Davenport. And Colonel Davenport had the good taste to stay decently out of the way. Quite unlike this."

"Hetty, you've gone too far," Tony said.

"Don't you dare." She took a step towards him as more heads turned in their direction from every side. "Don't you dare turn this on me. You've never taken your position seriously. You wouldn't be where you are if you hadn't had a wife smoothing the way for you."

"I don't deny it. But I never—"

"You never cared in the least for your position? So true. But you enjoyed the trappings of it enough. While you trampled all over every vestige of family honor—"

"How dare you!" Tony took a step forwards. "I've never forgot I'm a Southcott. You were willing enough to go along with the divorce—"

"I was making the best of things. Which I've learnt to do as your wife."

"You seemed to enjoy being duchess well enough."

"You're the one who dishonored the family."

"I never—"

Hetty pinned Tony with her gaze. "You're marrying a revolutionary."

"In fairness," Désirée said, "he did his best to outwit me for over two decades. It's not his fault that he didn't succeed more often."

"I succeeded a number of times," Tony said.

"Mmm. A few. There were some I didn't let you know about."

"Do be careful, my dear," Hetty said. "He gets dreadfully huffy when his pride is ruffled."

"You've noticed too?" Désirée turned to Hetty.

"Don't be absurd," Tony said.

"Bamford." Harry put a hand on Tony's arm. "People are staring."

He spoke the truth. Désirée could feel the force of the gazes directed at their box. One could only hope the diversion was working.

"Let them stare," Tony said.

"Do think of the children, Tony." Cordelia glanced towards Julien and Kitty's box, where her daughters Livia and Drusilla had joined Sophie, Colin, and Julien and Kitty's children. Hopefully enough of a crowd to compensate for Julien and Kitty's absence.

"Making such a fuss makes it worse for the children," Tony said. He turned to his wife. "You're the one who's always been too caught up in following the rules."

"I'm a woman. I had to."

"You're a duchess. You could get away with breaking them."

"Spoken like a man."

"Tony—" Désirée seized his arm. "You aren't being fair to your wife."

Tony spun towards her. "She called you a—"

"Well, one could argue she has a right. I've certainly disrupted her life."

"No, Tony's done that." Hetty's gaze moved to Désirée. "I pity you, my dear. He can seem so charming. He even charmed me for the first year or so. Then one starts to see he really lets nothing get in the way of his own comforts."

"I beg your pardon," Tony said.

"She does have a point," Désirée said.

"*What?*" he demanded.

"Oh, for god's sake, Tony. Your safe cottage is the definition of comfort."

"You were comfortable enough there yourself."

'Well, yes. I'm not going to turn up my nose at good wine and a soft bed."

"But you're too much of a revolutionary to admit you enjoy them?"

"If that isn't just like you," Hetty said. "Turning on her to protect yourself."

"I did nothing of the sort."

"You can't stop needling me about being a revolutionary," Désirée said. "It always got worse when I bested you."

"Tony hates to lose," Hetty said.

"Don't I know it," Désirée said.

"You aren't exactly a joy when you lose yourself," Tony pointed out.

"Don't be snappish, Tony."

"Be careful, my dear." Hetty took a step closer to Désirée. "He may be adventurous with a mistress. But things change a great deal when one marries. He has very definite ideas about being a duchess."

"I was afraid of that." Désirée shot a look at Tony.

"How on earth would you know?" Tony said to Hetty. "You were never my mistress."

"I should hope not. How dare you slander me? But I certainly know how you treat your mistresses."

"I'll never change," Désirée said. "That's why I resisted marriage for so long."

"Don't let Hetty bait you, darling." Tony put an arm round Désirée.

"He pretends he doesn't care about society," Hetty said, "but the truth is his life is built on society. You're a creature of society, Tony. You always will be."

Tony went still for a moment. As did Désirée. Tony's wife was a creature of society herself. She was also a very insightful woman.

CHAPTER 16

"Malcolm." The light, familiar voice stopped Malcolm as he made his way along the horseshoe corridor behind the boxes after delivering ices to the children. "I don't expect to see you out these days."

"I'm hardly a recluse." Malcolm smiled at Honoria Talbot Atwood. His childhood friend. And so much else that could not be put into words. "In fact, I'm less of one than I used to be." Damn. Any allusions to the past round Honoria were not safe ground.

"You don't go out in society. Much."

"This isn't society. It's the opera." Malcolm surveyed the corridor while keeping his gaze on Honoria. He'd been on his way to fetch champagne for Mélanie and make sure Kitty, Julien, Raoul, and Laura's disappearance wasn't drawing attention.

Honoria laughed. "Very clever."

"I wasn't trying to be clever. Gresham's a friend."

Her brows rose. "Since when?"

"Some time, actually. We have a number of friends in common. And his fiancée has been a friend for years."

"I forgot. Her brother's the Bow Street runner whom Judith married."

"Jeremy and Harriet Roth were friends of ours for years before that."

Honoria laughed, the same low, well-modulated laugh she'd had since childhood, and tilted her head to one side. "You always had unusual tastes, Malcolm."

"We're talking about friends."

"And you've always been determined to prove how broad-minded you were. I remember when the steward's son was your best friend."

"And he's now my brother-in-law."

"And a Bow Street runner is your cousin-in-law. You have an interesting family. But then so do I. I'm hardly one to comment." She laughed again, ruefully. "Did Tristram Gresham meet Miss Roth at your house?"

Dangerous ground. "I'm not sure where they first met. They share an interest in politics."

"Oh, Malcolm." Honoria tilted her head back. A ringlet fell against her cheek at a precise angle. "Only you could say a confirmed rake was interested in a woman because of politics."

"Most people have varied interests. Tristram Gresham is a number of things, but he certainly isn't conventional in his thinking or his actions."

"That's a charming way of putting it. I'm surprised you haven't tried to save her from him. But then you have ideas about women's independence. I suppose you don't want to interfere."

"Would you want anyone to interfere with your choice of marriage partner?" Damn. Dangerous ground again.

"You know I've always liked my own way. Though I haven't always got it." Her gaze caught and held his own. "You can't really think they can be happy together?"

"Who am I to say who may or may not be happy with

whom? I'm the last person to claim to be an expert on marriage."

"And yet you seem to believe in it now."

A dozen answers choked his throat. "I believe in the possibilities more than I once did, perhaps. I know the most wild-seeming risks can lead to happiness. I've seen it more times than I can count."

"Perhaps that was my mistake. Not taking enough of a risk. Odd. When I've always been one to run risks." She hesitated. "I can say that to you now. Good, perhaps, to be honest."

"Honesty is always good between friends."

"Is that what we are?" she asked.

"We've been friends since we were children."

"A lot's changed since we were children."

"Friendships last."

"You must have seen a dozen friendships strained. I can't imagine they go well with spying."

"You'd be surprised."

"You mean your circle of spy friends? Are you honest with them?"

"Surprisingly often. Though sometimes we're honest about lying."

"I don't deal in honesty, Malcolm. I think you know that now. It's oddly liberating to be able to say that. I spent so long trying to impress you."

"I don't need to be impressed."

"You say that, but you were horrified by the truth about me. Not but what I suspect you're far less of a stranger to secrets than I used to think. As a spy they must be your currency. And I imagine you deal with lies more than with honesty."

"It's unavoidable at times."

She smiled. "Perhaps I took quite the wrong tack with you. If I'd been open about my deceptions, I think you'd have been far more intrigued. Only look at whom you married."

Every instinct tensed. "There's no deception in my marriage."

"Malcolm. Mélanie's skills of every variety are quite apparent. It used to drive me mad that you married her when you resisted me, but I think I begin to understand."

Alarm shot through his senses. "I don't think anyone who knows Mélanie could fail to understand why I love her."

Honoria unfurled her silver spangled fan. "Believe me, Malcolm, I understand a great deal."

"MALCOLM."

Malcolm turned, having just extricated himself from Honoria, to look at the elegant features and clear blue eyes of Amelia Mallinson, wife of his former spymaster Hubert. "Lady Carfax."

She gave a tight smile that didn't reach her eyes. "I haven't been Lady Carfax for over a year, Malcolm."

Because Julien had returned from the dead and resumed the title that was rightfully his. Which Hubert had known all along was rightfully Julien's, as he had been blackmailing Julien into spying for him. Malcolm inclined his head. "Mrs. Mallinson."

"You'd better call me Amelia."

When Malcolm first became friends with David at Harrow, Amelia had welcomed him into her home. For a boy whose own home was anything but warm, it had meant a lot. "I'm happy to call you whatever you choose."

Amelia cast a quick glance round the corridor, as operagoers brushed past them. "I'm sorry to bother you." Her well-modulated voice trembled on the edge of cracking. "I didn't know where else to turn."

"Of course." Malcolm offered her his arm and drew her into a niche beside a bust of Athena that supported a brace of candles.

"Hubert can't know about this."

"You must know I have little difficulty keeping secrets from Hubert." Still he couldn't help but wonder what particular secrets Amelia wanted to keep.

Amelia drew in and released her breath. "It's Lucinda."

Lucinda had been sitting in the box with her parents during the first act, gaze trained on the stage. "Is she all right?" Malcolm asked.

"No—that is"—Amelia swallowed, glanced at the crowd in the passage, looked back at Malcolm—"she's eloped with Bernard Devereux."

Malcolm had a keen image of Lucinda and Bernard racing round the hedges at Carfax Court, both with scraped knees. "Are you sure?"

"Malcolm. I'm not a fool. Lucinda slipped out of the box at the start of the interval while I was talking to Lady London-derry. I thought she might be with Bernard, but I couldn't find him either. An obliging footman admitted to seeing them leave the theatre together, and I hope admits it no further. Lucinda must be brought back before this can spread."

"Lady—Amelia. Lucinda may be strong minded—she is, which I applaud—but she's never shown herself of a romantic disposition."

"Malcolm." Amelia fixed him with a firm gaze. "Surely I don't have to tell you, of all people, that romance can strike at unex-pected moments."

"Point taken. But Lucinda and Bernard have played together since they were Colin and Emily's age."

"One doesn't stay seven and eight forever."

"No, but it can be difficult to look on someone one grew up with through a romantic lens."

"That didn't seem to stop you and Honoria."

Malcolm bit back an instinctive denial. Easy enough to say

he'd never been remotely interested in Honoria. But not quite true. "Lucy's still—"

"Lucinda's been growing up. She was bound to, at some point. She's fought against it. Hubert indulged her. But I always knew at some point she'd take it seriously."

"Marriage?"

"She isn't taking marriage in the least seriously, judging by her behavior. Whyever she's disappeared with Bernard, she's risking ruin. You have to know that. How would you feel if it were Jessica?"

His daughter's bright-eyed gaze, fixed on the stage from her mother's lap, shot into Malcolm's mind. He could see them both, Mélanie's walnut brown ringlets brushing Jessica's pale blonde hair. "Concerned."

"So we have to get her back. Without Hubert knowing."

Malcolm raised a brow. "Hubert is a lot of things. But he can be helpful in a crisis."

"Malcolm, I don't know everything that's going on tonight, but it's quite plain something is. Hubert wouldn't have been so set on attending the opera otherwise. And if Hubert is pulled into this—he rarely makes a decision for personal reasons."

"I can't argue with that."

"It doesn't really even matter why she's left, in the end. You know what will happen if it gets out that she was gone with Bernard. Even for a few hours. And heaven help us if it's overnight. Lucinda may not take marriage seriously now, but some day she will want to marry. You know what this will mean for her. The endless talk. The raised brows. Forget Almack's— she won't be invited to the sort of parties that a woman like Cordelia Davenport can waltz through because she happened to already be married when she transgressed. Lucinda's already had her prospects changed by a scandal that wasn't of her making. She's gone from earl's daughter to earl's cousin, tainted by a scandal no one entirely understands about how Arthur—I mean Julien—was dead and then suddenly alive again. I don't want her options closed off further. I'll do everything to prevent that. You can't be such a Radical that you don't appreciate that."

"I hope I'll always appreciate the realities all of us are constrained to live with, however much I fight to change them."

"So you'll help me find her? We need to get her back. And come up with a story to explain her absence."

Malcolm pressed her hand. "You can't doubt I'd do anything for Lucinda."

"Thank you." Amelia cast a glance into the passage. "Where are Julien and Kitty?"

"I'm not sure." Malcolm kept his voice easy. "Getting a glass of champagne, I expect."

"You mean they've slipped off on a mission. Is it one Hubert knows about or one he doesn't? No, I don't expect you to tell me. But it's a pity. I'll admit Julien is handy in a crisis."

CHAPTER 17

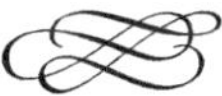

Raoul sidled up to the table where his quarry sat in the corner of the pub, moving across the ale-soaked floorboards with the careful steps of one who's had a pint or two too much. As he moved past, he stumbled and caught himself on the edge of the table. The table tilted under his weight. The half-full pint on it tipped over, spattering beer over the tabletop and dripping onto the floorboards. "Sorry, mate." Raoul rocked back on his heels. "Not usually so clumsy."

"No worries." The young man pushed his chair back from the table. He had a shock of light brown hair falling over a sharp-boned face. "I was on my way out."

"No, no." Raoul put out a hand. "Let me get you another pint."

The young man's brown eyes were bright and clear despite his evening in the pub. "No need—"

"It's the least I can do." Raoul pushed the young man back in his chair and lurched, catching himself on the half-timbered wall. "What are you drinking? Ale?"

"Bitter. But—"

"Capital. I'll have one myself." Raoul held up a hand to the barkeep. "Too early to call it a night."

"But—"

"Master home, is that it?"

"No, he's out," the young man said. "But—"

"Well, then." Raoul tossed a coin to the barkeep and he put two pints on the table. "At a ton ball, is he? Or Almack's?"

"Opera."

"Oh, that will go on for hours." Raoul held up his tankard. "Cheers."

"Cheers." The young man, whom Raoul had on good authority was John Southcott's valet, took a drink.

"Name's Bill Rourke," Raoul said. "Printer."

"I'm Tom Elton." Tom took a sip from his tankard. "Valet, as you seem to have guessed."

"You have the look of it." Raoul took a drink that was less deep than it appeared. "Difficult customer, is he? Your master?"

"No. Not really. Precise." Tom turned his pint on the table, circling the edges of a knot hole. "Likes things a certain way."

Raoul gave an understanding grunt. "One of those. Never could figure out how people stomach being in service. The pay's good, but being beholden to someone's whims—"

"It's not all bad. He's an important man. Brings dispatches home and the like. But he has his standards. Makes sense, in a position like his. But it's fair exhausting, I don't mind telling you, making sure everything is to his liking. I thought a bit ago he might be going to marry."

"Oh." Raoul slouched back in his chair and took a drink of bitter. "That can change a household."

"I thought this might make it better. She seemed a sensible lady. And we'd have expanded the staff. He'd have more people to—er—"

"Order about?"

"No. Yes. Well, perhaps." Tom pushed his tankard between

his hands. "No denying there's a lot to do. But it's enough to give one a headache trying to follow all his lists. Sometimes he has me redo things three or four times."

"You mean starching his cravats?"

"No—well, sometimes. And the times I've mixed boot polish again and again—you'd think the leather would have worn through in spots, I've redone the polish so many times. But more it's rewriting his notes of invitation, reordering his papers. He says it matters to get each detail right, but sometimes I can't but think wouldn't it be more useful if he just got on with things?"

"True, so much of the time. If you don't get on with things, you can't accomplish anything at all."

"Mmm." Tom tossed down a swallow from his pint. "We're late with everything. And then that makes him all the more worried. And then we end up scrambling about and inevitably there are mistakes. At least he's generous about evenings off. It's a bit of a relief, I don't have to tell you. Not worrying about every detail. Or what he'll say about every detail."

"Well, if he was thinking of marrying, perhaps he'll find someone else soon. Gentlemen often do when they have their mind set on marriage." Southcott's attachment to Harriet seemed surprisingly sincere, but he also was the sort who might make up his mind to marry and then make sure to find someone even if he lost his first choice.

"I don't think so—That is, he has, but she—" Tom stared into his pint.

Raoul leant back in his chair, tankard tilting from one hand, posture designed to give no hint how very interesting Tom's latest comment was. "Not the sort he'd likely marry? Gentlemen do often divide ladies up in categories."

"Yes. That is, I don't think it's that, precisely. I expect he would marry her if she weren't—" He broke off, flushing.

"If she weren't already married?" Raoul said. "That's often the way of it."

Which opened some very interesting questions about John Southcott.

❧

MALCOLM DROPPED down in a chair beside Mélanie, while Jessica, Emily, and Clara devoured a second round of ices David and Simon had fetched them before leaving to deliver more ices to Julien and Kitty's box next door. His posture was casual, but one look into her husband's eyes told Mélanie something had gone wrong. "Lucinda's missing," he murmured in a conversational tone, his back to the neighboring box where Lucinda's brother David was laughing with the children.

Mélanie kept her gaze steady on her husband's face and didn't risk a look round. "You know because—"

"Amelia told me. Apparently, a footman saw Lucy slip out with Bernard Devereux. Amelia's convinced they've eloped."

Lucinda's most trenchant comments on romance shot through Mélanie's memory. Along with fragments of Lucy's amiable squabbles with Bernard. "I'm sure they haven't eloped."

"So am I." Malcolm touched her shoulder. "Keep distracting everyone. I'll see what I can learn."

CHAPTER 18

*L*aura clung to the shadows of the area railing. A light step and a swish of skirts alerted her to someone coming down the street. A streetlamp gleamed off bronze ringlets escaping a chip straw bonnet, an upturned nose, and wide cheekbones. Maggie, who from advanced scouting they knew was the maid who looked after John Southcott, along with his valet Tom Elton. Who was now returning, inconveniently early, from her evening off.

Laura stepped out of the shadows with the quick walk of one in a hurry, gaze fixed on the cobblestones, arms tight round the stack of books she'd brought as a prop. She could feel the spectacles she'd added to her disguise slipping down her nose but resisted the impulse to push them in place. Better to appear as distracted as possible.

She collided with Maggie two doors down from John Southcott's lodgings and tumbled to the ground in a stage fall she'd learnt from actress and agent Manon Caret. The books tumbled from her arms onto the cobblestones.

"Oh, I'm so sorry!" Maggie had a light voice with an accent Laura thought was County Kerry. "Are you all right?"

"So stupid. I was thinking about tomorrow's lesson and not looking where I was going. Oh, dear, my spectacles." She ran a hand over the cobblestones, blinking as though to try to get her eyes in focus.

"Here they are." Maggie handed her the spectacles. "They don't seem to be cracked."

"Oh, thank goodness." Laura dusted the spectacles on her bombazine sleeve and pushed them back onto her nose. She began to gather up the books, but Maggie was already picking them up.

"I don't think they were damaged." Maggie smoothed the cover of one of the books. "Are you a teacher?"

"A governess." Laura reached for the books with one hand and tried to push herself up with the other. She slipped and landed back on her knees. A deliberate slip, but the pavement was still hard through the folds of her skirt.

"Here, let me." Maggie took the books and extended a hand to Laura.

"Thank you." Laura clambered to her feet, with little need to simulate wobbliness. "It's my evening out and I borrowed some books from a friend who's also a governess."

"I'm back from evening off too. I was seeing my parents."

"Agreeable to have family close." Laura took a half step and stumbled. "I'm afraid I've twisted my ankle."

Maggie glanced round. "The house where I work is two doors down. My master's rooms are on the second floor, but I have the use of the kitchen. It should be empty now. I could make you a cup of tea. You've had a fright."

"Oh, that would be lovely." Laura tightened her grip on the books. The kitchen should be far enough below John Southcott's lodgings that Maggie wouldn't overhear Julien and Kitty's break in. Especially with Laura distracting her.

Maggie took Laura's arm and helped her along the pavement two doors and then down the area steps and through a door that gave onto a typical London kitchen. Smaller than that in the Berkeley Square house, but not so very different. A stove, shelves of tins and crockery, a deal table in the center of the room. Maggie lit a lamp, helped Laura to a chair, and then went to poke up the coals in the stove. "It must be interesting to be a governess."

"Depends on the family you serve," Laura said, with truth from the days when she had indeed been a governess. "My present position's quite agreeable." She glanced round the kitchen. "Yours looks to be too. Though I know one can't always tell from surroundings."

"Oh yes." Maggie set a kettle on the stove, took a tin off a shelf, and began to spoon tea into a pot. "Mr. Southcott's a proper gentleman. Doesn't raise his voice. A bit exacting, and he does like things done a certain way. I do think it would be nice to be in a household with a family, though."

"Mr. Southcott's a bachelor?" Laura smoothed her skirts. The net of her opera dress scratched against the bombazine of the dress she'd put on over it.

"Yes, it's just me and Tom, his manservant, in the household." Maggie set two mugs beside the teapot. "A few weeks ago we did think Mr. Southcott might be about to marry. We weren't sure what that meant for our futures. But I'll own I quite liked the idea of a lady of the house. It doesn't seem to have come to anything, though. And now—" She broke off.

"He's too grief stricken to look at another lady?" Laura asked as the tea kettle shrilled. Oddly, in some ways she did think that might be true of John Southcott, when it came to Harriet.

"No. That is—" Maggie picked up the kettle and poured water into the teapot. "I don't think it will lead to marriage. I mean, it can't."

Interesting. And not what Laura had expected to hear of John Southcott. "Oh, your master has a mistress he wouldn't marry? Not surprising perhaps, if he's getting over this other girl. I hope it isn't a friend of yours?"

"Oh no." Maggie set the teapot on the table, and then the cups, and poured the tea. "She's not my sort at all. Quite a great lady, from what I can tell. She's only been here once and it was late at night. I just caught a quick glimpse of her. But she had her gloves off and I quite clearly saw she was wearing a wedding band."

Interesting indeed. Laura curled her hands round the cup of tea Maggie had given her. "You're sure she's Mr. Southcott's mistress?"

Maggie frowned as she seated herself across the table from Laura. "Well, Tom is sure she is. But I did wonder—Mr. Southcott's never had a woman visit him here before. And we know his work is fearful secretive. He's always making such a point of protecting his dispatch box. So I did wonder if perhaps the intrigue he and the lady were involved in wasn't romantic at all. But whyever she was meeting him, it was certainly secretive."

CHAPTER 19

"Where is she?" David pushed shut the curtains into Mélanie's box.

"Where is who?" Mélanie asked.

David cast a quick glance at the children, still absorbed in their ices. "My sister." He lowered his voice.

Mélanie met his gaze. "We aren't sure."

"Damn it." David's hands clenched. "But you know she's gone."

"Your mother told Malcolm."

"Why the hell didn't she tell us?"

"Your mother's a spy's wife." Simon put a hand on David's shoulder. "She knows to leave it to professionals."

David cast a sideways glance at his lover. "That's not funny."

"It wasn't meant to be funny."

"This is my sister." David spun back to Mélanie. "What happened?"

"We aren't sure. She seems to be with Bernard Devereux—"

"What—" David sucked in his breath and cast a quick glance round.

"Your mother was afraid they'd eloped—"

"Oh, that's one thing we don't have to worry about." The intensity in David's gaze lightened. "Lucinda's been pulling Bernard into scrapes since they could toddle. Ten to one that's what's happened now."

"Does she know what's happening tonight?" Simon asked, leaning casually with one hand on a chair back, gaze on Mélanie. "What's happening that you can't talk about?"

"Possibly," Mélanie said. "We didn't tell her, but she has keen instincts."

"And she spies on Father," David said.

"Quite," Mélanie said. "It wouldn't be the first time she tumbled to something."

David's gaze locked on Mélanie's own. "Assuming she did tumble to something, how much trouble is she likely to be in?"

Mélanie's fingers tightened on the folds of her gown. The instinct to protect her friends slammed against how much she knew she would want the truth if it were her younger sister—a fraught thought, considering her younger sister had died over decade ago—or her daughter. She cast a quick glance at Jessica, licking raspberry ice off her spoon. "We don't know. We don't know exactly what's going on. But Lucy has shown herself very capable in all sorts of situations."

"You can't tell me you aren't worried," David said.

"Oh, I'm terrified. For all sorts of reasons."

"JUST WHEN I thought you couldn't surprise me anymore." Honoria slipped through the door into the room off the green room that was given over to Tristram.

Tristram pushed himself to his feet from the desk where he'd been studying his marked-up score for the next act. "Talking of surprises, how did you get in here?"

A smile played about her mouth. "Surely you remember I can get just about anywhere I want."

"A fair point. But I fail to see how could I possibly surprise you?"

She folded her arms over the embroidered pearls and lace on her bodice. "I thought it was a mission, at first. It's quite clear you'll go to extraordinary lengths when you have an objective in mind. But then I saw the way you looked at her that day I met you on the street. Most rakes are romantics at heart."

"You aren't."

"Don't be so sure. I may have learnt my lesson, but there was a time I was quite convinced I could change my whole life round for love. I still wonder what would have happened if I'd had the chance to try."

"Rannoch would never have given you that chance."

Her carefully plucked and artfully penciled brows drew together. "He might have, if—"

"If you'd seduced him into it?"

"Marriages come about in all sorts of ways."

"Very true. Though some can start with insuperable challenges."

"I won't admit to that. But perhaps it's as well I married without any romantic illusions. I can't say I've ever been disillusioned with Atwood."

"And you think Harriet will be with me?"

"I wasn't talking about Harriet."

"My darling Honoria." Tristram leant back against the writing desk. "I have no illusions."

"That's nonsense, Tristram. You believe in all sorts of things. To a quite idiotic degree. I imagine your Miss Roth is much more sensible."

"Oh, Harriet's a thousand times more sensible than I."

"I suppose it's not surprising you fancy yourself in love with a woman who's so different from your other mistresses."

"I don't fancy myself anything."

"Tristram. You're so deep in the forest of illusions you can't see the sunlight anymore."

"And Harriet has never been my mistress."

Faint surprise flared in Honoria's eyes. "Spoken with chivalry."

"Spoken with truth."

She tilted her head to the side. "I should understand, I suppose. I thought it would be different if I'd married Malcolm. I've told him that. I've told myself that. But to you I can admit that most likely it wouldn't have been. People like you and me don't change. We can't resist the lure of a new challenge." She watched him a moment. "That's it, isn't it? She was a challenge. She didn't fall madly in love with you the moment you crooked your finger. She wouldn't tumble into bed with you without a ring on her finger."

"Don't be crude."

"You're the one who said she wasn't your mistress. And I can quite see it's an effective technique. Of course you'd want to find a way to win her. You'd go to any lengths. Even as far as the altar."

"There's another take, of course. That it has something to do with true love."

"Tristram, darling." Honoria took a step forwards into the spill of light from the brace of candles on the writing desk. "You're talking to me. Diamond cuts diamond. You don't think Malcolm fascinated me because he was a challenge? To you I can admit that. He was one of my few failures. I was willing to go to incalculable lengths. I was willing to go to the altar."

"You always intended to go to the altar eventually. It gives you more freedom."

"Perhaps. But I was so determined to win Malcolm I had myself convinced it would last. Only I have to admit now that once the challenge was done I'd have grown bored. I'd have wanted a new challenge. That's the thing about surrender. It can really only happen once. The longer the person holds out, the more intriguing the game. But the game still comes to an end with the surrender. You'll always be a game player, Tristram."

"The question would seem to be what type of game."

"We're both inveterate gamesters, my dear. And it's the oldest game possible."

"You make it sound tiresomely simple. I don't like simple."

Honoria tilted her head back. "That's not to say it can't be interesting to revisit old conquests. In fact, it's its own sort of excitement." She moved forwards and ran a hand down his arm.

Tristram jerked back. "No offense. But I have other interests now."

Honoria stared at him. He could see the flash of injured pride in her gaze. "Who is she?"

"Who is who?"

"You said yourself Miss Roth isn't your mistress. You can't tell me you've been living like a monk."

"Do you really think me so lacking in self-control?"

"I don't think 'control' is a word known to you. I won't tease you to tell me whom you've been amusing yourself with, but if you can dally with whoever it is, surely you can with me. For old time's sake."

Tristram regarded her. "I see."

"What?"

"I'm a challenge again."

"A challenge I conquered long ago. And actually, you weren't that much of a challenge."

"No, not then. I quite see that. But now I'm betrothed."

"Betrothed men aren't necessarily a challenge."

"Not unless they're determined to be faithful."

"That word sits oddly on you."

"If you didn't believe it, I don't think you'd be nearly so determined to rekindle things."

"Don't underrate yourself. You may not have been a challenge, but you did make things enjoyable."

"I'm going to be dull now. It may sound quixotic, but my interests have changed."

"They can't have changed *that* much. Unless you're ill."

"Some might call love a madness. But I don't feel ill."

"You can't tell me you've lost interest."

"Not in the least. My interests have just focused."

Honoria's eyes widened, then narrowed. "Once you've had her, they'll broaden again."

"I don't think so."

"Why? For god's sake, how can you sound so sure? You haven't even—"

"Don't be vulgar. It's nothing to do with that. I've never met anyone who thought so like I do."

"Oh, god. Have you become one of those people? Who claim to have discovered the delights of love and act as though everyone else should as well?"

"Oddly, Harriet once said much the same to me. But I'd never tell you to discover anything. I'd never claim to have answers for anyone. I only know what seems true for me."

"That you won't grow tired of a woman you barely know. In any sense of the word."

"I quarrel with you on barely know. In many ways, I know Harriet more intimately than I've ever known anyone. Though of course it's entirely possible she'll grow tired of me."

Honoria's fingers tightened on the sticks of her fan. "Don't be clever, Tristram."

"For once, I wasn't trying to be clever in the least."

"You'll grow bored once you've won the game. You'll realize she isn't nearly as fascinating as you think she is. You'll need a new challenge."

"It's not a game."

"Don't be silly, darling. Would you write the same opera

twice?" Her gaze went over his shoulder to the framed print for his first opera that hung on the wall. How ridiculously proud he'd been the day of the premiere. Prouder than he'd admit to anyone. "Your *Liliana* is quite different from your earlier work. You told me once you never wrote the same piece twice. That it would quite stifle your creativity."

"It's scarcely the same thing."

"No? You're a very creative lover, my dear. But you can't tell me you've never been bored. In fact, I think you've been more bored than you'll admit. Isn't that the reason you always ended a love affair?"

She had a point. Though mostly he'd ended a love affair when he'd secured the information he'd gone into it to uncover. "I've never claimed not to be able to change. In fact, I'm far more likely to change than to stay the same."

"Tristram—" Honoria broke off at a rap on the door.

"Sorry, Mr. Gresham." Matthew, the stage manager, poked his head through the door without waiting to be admitted. "But we're in a bit of a pickle."

MÉLANIE LOOKED ROUND as the curtains into the box stirred. She expected David and Simon had returned, but instead Tristram came through the curtains, gaze sharp with alarm.

"Malcolm?" Mélanie asked.

"No." Tristram shook his head. "At least, I haven't heard. But we have another problem. Danielle's missing."

"*What?*"

Tristram crouched down beside her chair, voice low and conversational, eyes shot with panic. "She was in the green room after act one. Then went to her dressing room. But she's not there now. No one can find her."

"She wouldn't have left for anything."

"No. I've raised the alarm. Meanwhile, we can't delay act two any longer. I need a Liliana."

Mélanie stared at him. "I'm a playwright. Sometimes an actress. Not—"

"I've heard you sing it. Especially the act two aria. The closest I've heard to Danielle. And you can own a theatre."

Panic shot through her. And a certain undeniable thrill. "Are you sure? Danielle's missing. I could help—"

"We'll find Danielle. We're all on it. But I need someone on stage to hold focus. Only you can do that."

"You're trusting me with a lot."

Tristram touched her shoulder. "I know you won't let me down."

CHAPTER 20

Malcolm paused beneath the colonnade in front of the King's Theatre and scanned the street. The footman—the same footman Amelia had spoken to—had admitted to seeing "a young lady in yellow and a young gentle-man" leave the theatre, but not to more. Carriages were drawn up in the street, two abreast, horses nodding their heads patiently and occasionally stamping their feet. Coachmen dozed on the seat, chatted with each other, sipped from flasks. Waiting for their masters and mistresses, who might choose to leave at any point in the performance to go to supper or make a late appearance at a ball or visit a gaming hell.

Malcolm stepped over a trail of wilting carnations that must have spilt from a flower seller's basket and studied the coach-men, wondering who might be the most observant and the quickest to talk. And then he saw him. A boy who looked about twelve, holding the reins of a pair of matched bays harnessed to a crested barouche with the wheels picked out in yellow. Malcolm crossed the pavement to him. "Filling in, are you? Coachman wanted to duck into a pub?"

"Nothing wrong with that." The boy met Malcolm's gaze, keeping his grip steady on the horses.

"Not in the least." Malcolm rubbed the nearest horse between the ears. "You're obviously careful with them. You have such keen instincts, I wonder if there are other things you saw tonight?"

"Like what?" The boy shifted his weight from one foot to the other.

"A young lady in yellow leaving the theatre with a young man about the same age."

Wariness shot through the boy's expression. "No reason for me to stop them. Plenty of people leave the theatre all the time. If I ever got to go to a play, I'd stay to see it through."

"Sensible of you. But did you happen to see where the young lady and gentlemen went? Even a direction they took along the street would help me."

The boy glanced from side to side.

Malcolm pulled his purse from inside his coat.

"Don't need to be paid to peach," the boy said.

"I admire your ethics. But I assure you I am concerned for their safety. And I won't report anything to the young lady's parents that she doesn't want them to know."

The boy drew in and released his breath. "I looked at them when they came out of the theatre in case this was their carriage. Thought I might have to summon the coachman right quick. But they went down the street and the young chap flagged down a hackney. It pulled up next to my—this carriage."

"Did you hear them say anything about the direction when they got in?"

"Oh yes. Clear as a bell. Funny how sound is sometimes. Number 10, Upper Brook Street."

Malcolm bit back a gasp. His mind shot in a dozen different directions, but he pressed a half crown and his card into the boy's hand. "Come round to my house in Berkeley Square tomorrow. We could use you in the stable."

The lad had quick ears. And if he had caught the address correctly, the night had taken its oddest turn yet.

THE STAIRS to John Southcott's lodgings creaked less than those to Bertram Caulfield-West's. Julien moved quietly but not hurriedly, Kitty beside him. If any of the other lodgers saw them, they were just calling on a friend. The trickiest part was when they got to Southcott's door. Raoul and Laura could certainly be trusted to keep the valet and maid occupied, but difficult to explain why Julien was kneeling at the door with a picklock and his ear to the keyhole. Kitty stood with her skirts spread wide to conceal him.

The lock took a few tries but was not a real challenge. Julien turned the handle and eased the door open onto a dark room. Minimal light from the windows. Dark blurs of furniture. And one—

Julien put himself in front of Kitty. And then ran forwards as two shadowy blurs rushed him. He was off balance and out of practice, but he sent one man flying across the room and knocked the other to the ground. He dropped down on the second man's chest and grabbed the lapels of his coat.

"Stop," the man yelled. "I'm a Bow Street officer."

CHAPTER 21

*J*ulien sat back on his heels but kept his grip on the man's lapels. "Anyone could say that."

Lamplight flared, spilling over the floorboards and revealing a red-haired man in a dark coat on whose chest Julien was presently sitting, and another with brown hair lying across the room at an awkward angle while Kitty bent over him and held a knife to his throat.

"Lord Carfax." Another voice spoke from the shadows. Incisive and familiar. "You just assaulted two of my officers."

Julien released his hold on the red-haired man and met the gaze of the chief magistrate of Bow Street. "Sir Nathaniel. Your officers attacked Lady Carfax and me. Our instinct was naturally to fight back." Julien extended a hand to the man he'd knocked down. "No hard feelings."

Kitty straightened up, tucked the knife back into her reticule, and offered a hand to the other officer. He got to his feet, a wary eye on her, and then sketched an awkward bow. Kitty nodded as though they were meeting in a drawing room and pulled a flask from her purse. "Perhaps you'd like some? Julien has a rather punishing left."

The officer hesitated, cast a glance at the chief magistrate, then took a quick drink.

"I assume you and Lady Carfax had your reasons for breaking into Mr. Southcott's rooms in the middle of the night," Sir Nathaniel Conant said.

"Who said we broke in?" Julien ran a hand over his hair.

"You picked the lock."

"We both pick locks all the time." Kitty offered the flask to the other officer. "Mr. Southcott's uncle, the Duke of Bamford, is one of our dearest friends, as I'm sure you know, Sir Nathaniel. The duke asked us to break in and leave a surprise for Mr. Southcott."

Conant's brows drew together. "What surprise?"

"A special drawing by his daughter." Kitty pulled a drawing of a puppy out of her reticule. Timothy had drawn it, not Tony and Désirée's daughter Sophie, but it was unsigned.

Conant frowned down at it. He might not be possessed of a huge amount of imagination, but he could recognize a story. Still, Kitty had managed just enough truth in it that he couldn't openly call them liars. At least, not given that they were Earl and Countess Carfax. Julien detested how the title his worthless father had left him could at times be so very useful.

"Er—charming," Conant said.

"Yes, isn't it?" Kitty said. "It's of her puppy." Actually, it was of the new Mallinson family puppy, but for all his intelligence sources presumably Conant wasn't keeping notes on various people's dogs.

"Just so," Conant said. "But I don't quite see—"

The door burst open.

"Conant, have you got them?"

The booming voice belonged to Lord Sidmouth, the home secretary. Julien recognized it before Sidmouth strode through the door and went still at the sight that met his eyes. So did the slighter man beside him, Lord Londonderry, the foreign secretary. Whom Julien would always think of as Lord Castlereagh despite his new title.

"I don't understand," Sidmouth said. "Where are the perpetrators?"

Castlereagh's cool blue gaze skimmed over Julien and Kitty, then settled on Conant. "I believe they are in front of us. Sidmouth and I were sent word that Bow Street planned to intercept two dangerous foreign agents in the midst of stealing government secrets tonight. I don't believe I see any foreign agents here."

"I was born in Spain," Kitty said. "And I was an agent. Ask Hubert Mallinson."

"There seems to have been a misunderstanding," Conant said. "Lord and Lady Carfax were delivering a message to Mr. Southcott."

"A message?" Sidmouth asked.

"A drawing from his cousin." Kitty held out the drawing.

Sidmouth peered at it in the lamplight. His brows rose.

"Made by Bamford's youngest, I presume," Castlereagh said.

"Lady Rosalind?" Sidmouth asked in surprise.

Castlereagh coughed. "I believe he and Mademoiselle Clairineau have a daughter."

"Sophie." Kitty's smile was brighter than a dozen wax tapers. "She's charming. And such a good artist and so fond of her puppy. She's taken such a liking to her cousin John. So sweet. She wanted the drawing to surprise him when he came home tonight—she knows how hard he's been working. Julien and I offered to get the drawing to him. Sophie was so impressed when she learnt we could pick locks."

Castlereagh regarded Kitty. Julien wasn't sure how much he knew about her work in the Peninsula and the Argentine, but he knew she'd been an agent for Hubert. And Hubert was not one of Castlereagh's favorite people. His gaze shifted to the drawing, almost as though he were checking for a coded message. "A talented child. But then her mother is very talented."

Désirée Clairineau's talents and what they'd led to, and could still lead to, hung in the air.

"So she is," Julien said. "A divorce is always challenging for a family, but John Southcott certainly appreciates the brilliance of the woman his uncle is marrying."

"Southcott doesn't strike me as the sort to be fond of a French agent," Sidmouth said.

"It's wonderful what family feeling can do," Kitty said with a bright smile. "There was a time when I never thought my husband and Uncle Hubert would be on good terms."

Sidmouth coughed.

"Mr. Southcott understands what Désirée means to his uncle," Kitty said. "In fact, he has a great appreciation for it. He understands some things come before politics."

Sidmouth peered at the drawing again, then glanced round the company with a scowl. "It's all very well, but if Lord and Lady Carfax broke into Southcott's rooms to leave him a surprise gift, who alerted us and Bow Street?"

"I can't know." Julien leant a hand on a pier table with a casual sprawl that he hoped would lend an appropriate touch to the scene. "But I suspect someone was playing a trick on us."

"My husband is being charitable," Kitty said. "I'm quite sure it was one of our younger cousins. They do like causing mischief."

"Which cousins?" Castlereagh asked.

Kitty sighed and exchanged a look with Julien.

"I think we have to admit it," Julien said.

Kitty nodded. "As perhaps you know, our cousin Lucinda feels terribly confined on the marriage mart, and is always longing to be part of the family intrigue. I confess we've caught her listening at keyholes more than once"—that was true—"and I'm sure there's more we don't know about. She's a dear girl and

I do think if she had something more concrete to do with her energies she wouldn't get up to such pranks—"

"You think Lucinda Mallinson summoned us and Bow Street as a prank?" Sidmouth demanded on a note of incredulity.

"Well, can you think of another explanation?" Kitty asked, wide-eyed.

"No. That is—"

"I'm sure she didn't realize it would go so far," Kitty said.

"You're being charitable," Julien said. "The truth is, much of the time Lucinda doesn't think at all. If she could go on a proper spy mission, she might have some understanding of what she's meddling in. Perhaps—"

"Oh no, darling," Kitty said. "You'd drive Uncle Hubert and Aunt Amelia to distraction. And Lucinda wouldn't have the least idea how to take care of herself."

"My feckless cousin," Julien said, "has always been very well able to take care of herself. It's other people who don't fare so well when she gets up to her antics."

Kitty sighed and looked from Conant to the two officers to Castlereagh and Sidmouth. "I'm so sorry for all the trouble you've been caused."

"Odd," Conant said. "John Southcott himself sent the warning to Bow Street."

"Well, of course," Kitty said, eyes very wide. "How better to play a trick on us than to warn Mr. Southcott and have him warn you to be lying in wait for us?"

Julien examined his nails. "This is the sort of prank families of spies get up to."

"Lucinda does like to tease John," Kitty said. "I can't but wonder if it means she has a tendre for him, though of course she'd deny it."

Julien sent his wife a look.

Kitty's answering look was at once a silent apology to Lucinda and a statement that Lucinda would be the first to understand. Which was probably very true. "Not the match I'd choose for my cousin," Julien said. Also quite true. "Though of course she's free to choose for herself." Again very true.

"You're saying we've been caught up in some young girl's romantic games?" Sidmouth asked.

"I'm so sorry," Kitty said. "I'm afraid the Mallinson family can't steer clear of intrigue of all sorts."

CHAPTER 22

The footman at Number 10 Upper Brook Street regarded Malcolm with surprise beneath the fanlight over the Ionic portico. "Mr. and Mrs. Atwood are from home, Mr. Rannoch."

"Yes, I know." Malcolm removed his hat and held it out with the assumption that he'd be allowed to enter. "But I think Miss Lucinda is here?"

The footman blinked. "I'm not sure—"

"Malcolm." Lucinda swept down the stairs into the marble-tiled hall, Bernard Devereux trailing in her wake. "What a stroke of luck. I'm so glad to see you." She flashed a smile at the footman. "Thank you, Gerald. No need to tell Mrs. Atwood I was here. She'll rag me forever if she realizes I left my fan behind for the third time. She says I can't keep track of anything."

"Well, in fairness, Luce, you often can't," Bernard murmured.

"Oh, don't you start, Bernard." Lucinda tossed her head. "You're as bad as Honoria." She smiled at the footman again. "Do enjoy your evening, Gerald. I expect they won't be back from the opera for ages. It's quite riveting. You will escort us back, won't you, Malcolm?"

"Of course." Malcolm set his hat back on his head.

"Here now." Bernard's voice rose with affront. "I escorted you."

"Well, yes. But there's no denying Malcolm's a grown-up." Lucinda linked her hands through Malcolm's and Bernard's arms as they descended the steps.

"Sorry, Rannoch," Bernard murmured as the door swung shut behind them. "And sorry for the bit about forgetting things, Lucy. I thought it might help with distraction if I seemed the biggest idiot possible. Though you have forgot things more than once."

"Oh shush, Bernard. Though you're right, we needed to look as silly as possible." Lucinda looked up at Malcolm. "I think we have them."

Malcolm paused on the pavement and regarded her in the glow of a streetlamp. It didn't seem so very many years ago that he'd carried her about on his shoulders. "Have what?"

"The papers you've all been trying to get back and Papa's glowering over." Lucinda smiled up at Malcolm, eyes bright in the lamplight. "You do know I'm good at listening."

"Yes, but—" Malcolm glanced up at the cool cream sandstone of the house behind him. The house where Honoria had lived since she'd married Atwood.

"Oh, I suppose you're surprised I found them when all of you seasoned spies couldn't," Lucinda said. "But honestly, I had a huge advantage." She followed Malcolm's gaze to the house. "I mean, I don't think any of you knew that John Southcott is having an affair with Honoria."

Julien turned his head to look at Kitty as they made their way from Southcott's lodgings back towards the theatre. Over a decade knowing her, a year and a half married to her, and she could still surprise him. "You were brilliant."

"Which got us out of Southcott's rooms but doesn't get us any closer to Southcott's papers." Kitty glanced at him in the yellow glow of a streetlamp. "Southcott set us up. When he came into Berkeley Square with his threats, he wasn't just trying to keep us quiet. He was setting up this. He even made a point of mentioning that he'd be at the *Liliana* premiere."

"Yes." Southcott's expression that night in Berkeley Square danced before Julien's eyes. "He's more enterprising than I credited. Which means the papers almost certainly aren't in his rooms. And makes me wonder what else he had set up."

Kitty shivered.

Julien tightened his grip on her arm. "We'll find them."

"We'll manage for Leo. It's worse for Archie. Harry's trying to be calm, but it could force Archie and Frances from the country."

"All the more reason why we have to find the papers. It's not as though we've never faced a high-stakes mission before."

They reached the King's Theatre, flashed their box tokens at the footmen, and crossed to the grand staircase. They were halfway up one of the staircases to the boxes, when a clear, carrying voice echoed into the semicircular stairwell. Julien went still. "That sounds like—"

They took the rest of the stairs two at a time and went into their box. To be greeted by smiles from their children and the Davenport girls and Sophie. Colin was also in the box, but he didn't look round. His gaze was riveted on the stage. Where his mother was delivering the last line in Liliana's aria.

❧

"No one saw Danielle leave the building," Harriet said to her brother. "Not the stage manager, not the backstage doorman, not the footmen in the lobby. And Danielle wouldn't leave in the midst of a performance. I think she's still here."

Jeremy nodded. They were in a passage backstage. The orchestra, conducted by Tristram, and Mélanie, singing Danielle's role, echoed from the stage. Chorus members in varying stages of dress, and dressers with their arms full of costumes and their mouths full of pins, hurried past them. Clouds of powder and the smell of greasepaint hung in the air.

Harriet turned her head at a faint sound. Jeremy's gaze went in the same direction. Of one accord, they moved towards the sound. Thudding. It grew louder as they approached. From the locked door of a storage room just down the passage from Danielle Darnault's dressing room. Harriet tried the door handle. It was locked. "Danielle?" she said.

"Yes." Danielle's voice, low-pitched but clear. "I'm trying not to shout."

Harriet glanced round the passage.

"Give me a hairpin," Jeremy said. "Picking the lock's quicker than finding someone with a key."

Jeremy had the lock open in under a minute. Danielle Darnault stepped into the passage, wrapped in a cherry silk dressing gown, hair already twisted into the style for act two, though it was slipping from its pins. Harriet put a hand on her arm. "What happened?"

"I'm not sure. But I think my tea was drugged in the interval. I remember looking into the mirror and then everything going wobbly. I woke up in the closet." She turned towards the sound from the stage. "Is—"

"Mélanie went on," Harriet said. "But you can do act three. If—"

"If I have the voice for it," Danielle said. "Give me a few minutes and some salt water."

CHAPTER 23

"Honoria slipped out of the drawing room at Mama's reception last week." Lucinda looked round the crowd gathered in the Berkeley Square library, which included Hubert and Amelia. Given the events of the night, Mélanie had thought it best to include everyone in the explanations. Malcolm had been quick to agree. "I could tell something was up, so I followed her," Lucinda continued. "She went into Papa's study, of all places. And I know precisely the best spot to overhear conversations in there."

"Thank you," Hubert murmured.

"You can't tell me you don't know I overhear things," Lucinda said.

"Not to that extent," Hubert said.

"I probably shouldn't have let you on to it." Lucinda regarded the man who was Britain's unofficial spymaster and her father. "But in any case, I overheard Honoria with Mr. Southcott. No, not doing that," she added quickly at a gasp from her mother and some raised brows from others. "They were just talking. But it was quite clear what their relationship was. And I also heard Mr. Southcott tell Honoria he needed her to keep some papers for him. Only I didn't realize what those papers might be or how important they were until I overheard Mr. Southcott talking to Papa a couple of days ago."

Hubert put his head in his hands.

"Don't take it so hard, Uncle Hubert." Julien put a hand on his uncle's shoulder. "I expect Leo and Timothy—or Genny—will be pulling the wool over Kitty's and my eyes in no time."

"I suppose I could have told you all." Lucinda cast a glance round the room. "But I wanted to show what I could do. And honestly, I think it may have been easier for me to get into Honoria's house without rousing suspicion than if I'd involved the rest of you."

"Honestly," Malcolm said, "I think you were right."

"What about Danielle?" Cordelia asked. "Who drugged her?"

"I think Honoria and Southcott set it up," Tristram said. He was on the sofa beside Harriet, still basking in the glow of a successful performance. "And then Honoria dragged Danielle into the closet before she came to see me backstage. She'd just have had to wait for a moment when the passage was empty. If anyone had spotted her backstage, she'd have said she was looking for me."

"Drugging Danielle didn't really add anything to Mr. Southcott's plan to entrap everyone with the papers," Judith said.

"No," Tristram agreed. "I think that was directed purely at me. Southcott's a cool strategist, but as we've seen, he isn't without personal feelings." He cast a quick glance at Harriet.

"I never—" Harriet said.

"No. But Southcott had hopes. He didn't like losing you. He particularly didn't like losing you to a reprobate like me who also happens to be a Radical."

"Not to mention Honoria Atwood didn't like losing you to an insignificant nobody," Harriet added.

"Say what you will of Honoria, she's too clever to see you as a nobody, my sweet. But yes, she wanted revenge as well. So

Honoria and Southcott attempted to bring down the opening. And failed, thanks to Mélanie."

"More thanks to Harriet and Jeremy for getting Danielle out so she could finish the performance," Mélanie said, petting Browne in her lap. Though to herself she could admit it had been exhilarating to go on for those few scenes.

"I'm sorrier than I can say for what happened to Danielle," Tristram said. "And I'm inestimably glad she got to finish the performance. But I'll never forget hearing you sing act two."

Mélanie smiled at him. It meant far more than she could put into words.

"Every time I think I start to understand John, the image shifts," Harriet said.

Raoul met her gaze, his own level yet quietly kind as it could be. "For what it's worth, from my talk with Southcott's valet, I think his entanglement with Honoria Atwood was quite recent. And however much Southcott may have misread your own feelings, he does seem to have been quite sincere in hoping to marry you."

Laura nodded. "Maggie, the maid I spoke with, said much the same. Mr. Southcott is a complicated person. A dangerous person. But not without feeling."

"I go cold thinking of what he could have done," Harriet said.

"My nephew is an even more dangerous man than I realized," Tony said.

"Strategy seems to run in the family." Désirée put her hand over Tony's own. "Which isn't always helpful. We forget sometimes that the other side can be as clever as we can. And they have allies too."

Harry looked at Lucinda. "Everyone here owes you a debt of gratitude." He wasn't explicitly going to mention his uncle Archie in front of Hubert.

"I'm glad you have the papers back," Lucinda said. "But I don't think the curtain's fallen on Mr. Southcott. Or Honoria."

"On the contrary." Julien reached for his whisky and stared into the glass. "I'm quite sure this is just the prologue."

～

"You'd think by now I'd be used to surprises from Honoria." Malcolm pushed the door to the nursery to, and paused, staring down at his shirt cuffs.

Mélanie walked up behind her husband and slid her arms round him. "This was hard to see coming. Though in retrospect, perhaps it's not surprising."

Malcolm turned in her arms and looked down at her, hands on her shoulders, brow raised.

"Honoria always struck me as the sort who'd have been a splendid diplomat or a politician or a general, if such roles were open to women," Mélanie said. At least, that was how she'd seen Honoria Talbot Atwood once she'd got over seeing her as the perfect wife Malcolm might have married if he'd been free. "Romantic intrigue offers a sort of power. But perhaps it's no wonder she turned to raw political power."

"Through Southcott." Disbelief echoed in Malcolm's voice.

"I know it must be hard to imagine a woman who once wanted you wanting John Southcott—"

"Mélanie—"

"You wouldn't be human if you didn't feel it, darling. But I think we have to accept that John Southcott is even more adept than we realized after our last investigation. And it's going to take all our ingenuity to fight him."

"And Honoria," Malcolm said.

"And Honoria," Mélanie agreed. Aware of how much it cost him to say it. Aware of how much the coming months were going to cost all of them.

Malcolm bent his head and kissed her. "Good thing we all know what it is to live in a crisis."

135

THE PICCADILLY RECKONING

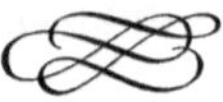

Malcolm and Mélanie Rannoch's adventures
in espionage and investigation continue
in Tracy Grant's new historical mystery
On sale May 2026

London
October 1821

"It doesn't quite work now that I see it play out on stage." Mélanie Rannoch turned to Simon Tanner at the table they were sharing on stage at the Tavistock Theatre, watching an early rehearsal of her new play. "We need something stronger to get them to this point."

"It works." Simon leant back in his chair and stretched his arms over his head. "But I agree it can be stronger."

"If you want my opinion," Brandon Ford said, getting up from the table where the cast had been reading through the script, "it's because it isn't clear enough why he doesn't want to lose her. At the same time, if he really doesn't want to lose her, he's a right idiot to take such risks."

"And he doesn't in the least understand what matters to her," Manon Caret added, staring down at her script. "Which makes for good drama. But the stakes have to be clear when she finally leaves him. I mean, I know it's not finally, but it needs to feel like that at this point."

"Right," Mélanie said. "But I didn't see it until now. You both bring it to life in a way it can't be in my head."

"That's the point of rehearsal." Simon pushed himself to his feet. "Tea, I think. It's always easier to think—"

He broke off at the sight of a man coming down the main aisle of the theatre. Mélanie turned and went still at the sight of the distinctive red waistcoat of the Bow Street patrol. Simon went still as well, as did Manon and Brandon. The Tavistock's involvement in Radical politics suggested all sorts of possible reasons why Bow Street might put in an appearance at the theatre.

As the patrol approached, Mélanie recognized the round face and red hair of Dawkins, who worked with their friend, Bow Street runner Jeremy Roth. Less likely he'd come to arrest someone. But still concerning. "Dawkins?" she called. "What is it?"

"I'm sorry, Mrs. Rannoch. Mr. Tanner." Dawkins came to a stop at the edge of the stage and looked up at them in the dusty light. "Mr. Roth sent me. He's hoping Mrs. Rannoch can come with me. There's been an explosion outside a pub in Piccadilly."

ROGER SMYTHE SET his glass of port down and stared at the notes strewn on the table. "We're never going to pass this. One wonders why we're trying at all."

Malcolm Rannoch looked at Roger and his other colleagues gathered round the table in a private room at Brooks's, the

London club that was the domain of the Whigs. "We're making a point. We're chipping away round the edges."

"And you think all that chipping is getting us somewhere?" Roger asked.

"I do. It's what keeps me going," Malcolm said. Not that he didn't have doubts at times. But he wasn't going to share those with his younger colleagues whose focus he needed.

Roger turned his glass in his hand. "I'm drinking port round a table in a club. I feel like I've turned into my father. Save that he'd have been at White's not Brooks's."

"Don't think Brooks's versus White's doesn't make a difference," Rupert Caruthers said. "And don't think I haven't had the same thoughts about my father."

"You're neither of you like your fathers," Malcolm said.

"Whereas you're very like O'Roarke," Roger said. "Which is what I'd want if he were my father. Is he really going to stand for parliament?"

"I think so." Malcolm was still careful when it came to navigating the changes in his father's life, changes he had helped bring about. "If—"

He broke off as the door opened and a footman came into the room, holding a silver salver with a note on it. "I'm sorry to interrupt, Mr. Rannoch. But this was just delivered from a Mr. Roth of Bow Street. The lad who delivered it says it's urgent."

MÉLANIE SMELT the sulfur tang of smoke even before she turned into Piccadilly. She saw the glow as she rounded the corner. The carriage, drawn up in front of the Rose & Crown, was still smoldering. Embers glowed on what had been the seats. Bits of yellow on the wheels showed through the soot. The two front windows of the Rose & Crown had shattered. Glass and soot and debris littered the pavement between the pub and the carriage.

Two tall men turned at her approach and came towards her. Jeremy and Malcolm. Thank god Jeremy had reached Malcolm as well.

"Thank you for coming." Jeremy was bare-headed, smears of soot on his face and shirt collar and cravat. The glow from the embers flashed in his eyes. "I saw explosions set with mines in the Peninsula. I've never encountered anything quite like this in London."

"Casualties?" Mélanie glanced between the two men at the wreckage of the carriage.

"One dead." Roth pulled out his notebook. "Sir Stephen Strangeways. I understand from Malcolm he's a politician."

"A Tory backbencher," Malcolm said. His gaze was dark, with a fear that went beyond the death of a distant colleague. "I'd met him once or twice but can't claim to have known him well, as I've been telling Jeremy."

"You said 'one dead,'" Mélanie said, stomach tight from the fear in Malcolm's gaze and what it might imply. "There are others injured?"

Malcolm's jaw tightened, but he waited for Jeremy to speak.

"They're both inside, unconscious," Jeremy said. "We've sent for a doctor. One of the wounded is Baron Josef Hauke, from the Austrian embassy. I understand Malcolm knows him."

"We both do." Mélanie said. In fact, Hauke had abducted Malcolm in the course of a recent investigation to share information. Partly at Malcolm's instigation, so she couldn't really blame Hauke. "And?"

Jeremy drew in and released his breath.

Malcolm put a hand on Mélanie's arm and said a name that nearly sent her tumbling to the pavement in the sort of collapse that should have been beneath her. "Julien."

THE DUKE'S GAMBIT

SECRETS OF A LADY

THE MASK OF NIGHT

THE DARLINGTON LETTERS

THE GLENISTER PAPERS

A MIDWINTER'S MASQUERADE

THE TAVISTOCK PLOT

THE CARFAX INTRIGUE

THE WESTMINSTER INTRIGUE

THE APSLEY HOUSE INCIDENT

THE WHITEHALL CONSPIRACY

THE SEVEN DIALS AFFAIR

THE ACKERLEY INHERITANCE

THE O'ROARKE AFFAIR

THE GRESHAM SCANDAL

THE COVENT GARDEN CAPER

ACKNOWLEDGMENTS

This novella was written over a very busy summer, including many late nights at rehearsals and performances. Theatre and opera always inspire me. In this case, theatrical and musical inspiration drove the story. As always, huge thanks to my wonderful agent, Nancy Yost, for cheering the Rannochs on and for her keen insights and brilliant eye editing cover copy. Thanks to Natanya Wheeler, a fabulous Director of Digital Rights, for shepherding the book expertly through each stage of the publication process and creating another brilliant cover that captures Mélanie Rannoch and the mood of the story. To Sarah Younger for helping the book along through production and publication, and to Sarah and Christina Miller for superlative social media support. To Valentina Boré for the beautiful character and quote cards. And to the entire team at Nancy Yost Literary Agency for their fabulous work. Their creativity and dedication make all of them a dream to work with. Malcolm, Mélanie, and all the other characters and I are very fortunate to have their support.

Thank you to Eve Lynch for the meticulous and thoughtful copyediting. I love sharing the Rannochs with you and so appreciate your care for getting their story right when it comes to everything from historical usage to series continuity.

Thank you to Kristen Loken for a magical author photo. Your brilliance never fails to amaze me, Kristen!

I am very fortunate to have a wonderful group of writer friends near and far who make being a writer less solitary.

Thanks in particular to Lauren Willig for sharing the joys of historical research and the challenges of juggling life as a writer and a mom. To Penelope Williamson, for sharing wonderful writer escapes to the Oregon Shakespeare Festival and the Oregon coast, during one of which this novella was finished, and hours of inspiring talk. Thank you to the #momswritersclub for bimonthly chats that are energizing and inspiring, and especially to Shay Galloway, with whom I co-host the chats, and to Jessica Payne for starting the group.

Thank you to the readers who support Malcolm and Mélanie and their friends and provide wonderful insights on my website and social media, and especially on the Goodreads Discussion Group for the series.

Thanks to Gregory Paris and jim saliba for creating and updating a fabulous website that chronicles Malcolm and Mélanie's adventures.

And thank you to my daughter Mélanie, for brainstorming *The Covent Garden Caper* (including key action sequences), proofreading, and supporting me all the way through the process, during a particularly busy time in our lives. I am so proud she is now writing herself—and also singing and acting, which tie right into this story. From the time she could touch the keys, Mélanie has contributed something to each of my books. This is Mélanie's contribution to this story – "Throughout the years, mom has written tons of incredible books, and I hope that you enjoyed this one, Reader. When I was little I remember I had no idea why mom was letting me type, but very much enjoying hitting every button on the keyboard. Now, I struggle to think of words that properly describe how much I love my mom, and how proud I am of her. She is so so incredible, amazing, wonderful, astonishing, inspiring, all the words. Every single word that could mean most incredible person in the universe means my mom. I love you, mummy!"

ABOUT THE AUTHOR

Photo Credit: Kristen Loken

Tracy Grant studied British history at Stanford University and received the Firestone Award for Excellence in Research for her honors thesis on shifting conceptions of honor in late-fifteenth-century England. She lives in the San Francisco Bay Area with her daughter, four cats, and a gecko. In addition to writing, Tracy is Executive Director of Cantare, **an organization dedicated to sharing the power and beauty of choral music through adult choirs, youth programs, and concert performances.** Her real-life heroine is her daughter Mélanie, who is very supportive of Mummy's writing and has become a writer herself. Tracy is currently at work on her next book chronicling the adventures of Malcolm and Mélanie Rannoch. Visit her online.